Like a Reed in the Wind

Short Stories, Poems, Skits and Devotionals

I0630221

By Randy Colver

ISBN 978-0-615-32727-3

Contents

Introduction

"What did you go out into the desert to see?
A reed swayed by the wind?"—*Jesus Christ*

John the Baptist was a voice for his generation—a voice of preparation calling the people of Judea to repentance. Few attain to such a purpose. Most are content to sway with the winds of this world, their voices drowned out by the noise of countless, blustery opinions.

A few of us are mere echoes of the prophet's words of truth, carrying forward to new generations what is of eternal value. On these pages are bits and pieces of the sounds of a message as true today as it was two thousand years ago: "The kingdom of heaven is at hand."

John was a hardened oak, resisting his world in his time. My prayer is that you may find these words, as his, to be fun, moving, Christ-centered, and sometimes more than a reed in the wind.

—the Author

A Prayer to the Father

What is this that you have done,

That you would give your only Son?

Who can count the price you paid,

When on his back those stripes were laid?

Did your heart most surely break,

For him whose cross you did forsake?

But was there joy when three days on,

He rose to meet that glorious dawn?

Oh, that I might learn to give,

To suffer well that I might live,

And learn to trust when all is lost,

Recounting all his life did cost.

So to the hills I lift my eyes,

To the Helper of my desires,

To him who gave his only Son,

Who shares the joy that has begun.

Lepers among Us

DO YOU REMEMBER the movie Ben Hur? Remember the remarkable scene where the hero (played by Charleton Heston) saw the leper colony for the first time and was gripped by the monstrous inhumanity to these outcasts of society? In a very moving scene, he ignores the personal dangers and heads hell-bent deep into the caves searching for his leprous sister, Tirzah. When he finds her, he gathers her in his arms—despite her protests—to bring her home. One would be hard-pressed to find a better illustration of Christ, who searched for us in the dark recesses of sin and rescued us from estrangement from the Father.

But there are, even now, those in the Church who are lepers. You know them, the peculiar ones—the ones that no one wants to be around, let alone befriend. They have tattoos, or can't hold a job. They are obese, loud, or generally obnoxious. Constantly negative. A different color. A different smell. And we treat them like lepers. We avoid them, and justify it with high-sounding words: "You become who you spend time with." We don't go after them. We don't invite them to our small group. They make us uncomfortable.

But Christ, alone among all those of the crowd, reached out his hand to touch the leper. No glove—just bare skin against raw, open sores. How rare that must have been for the leper—the soft touch—the hand of compassion—the hand of healing! Here was the Good Shepherd leaving the ninety-nine to find the lost one.

Not long ago I began to look around for those who weren't in any small group, but quickly realized all the "good" ones were taken. That's when I noticed them: *the lepers among us.* So I gathered them. "You are the first one to ask me," remarked one such brother, who has attended our church for years. And so it was that I became a leper. For when you associate with lepers, you are avoided, too. Guests have come to our "colony," observed the lepers, and left. I don't blame them. It's hard for most people. They want to go to a small group where they can be encouraged, not deal with a disease. You must love the unlovely to be a part of this one.

My wife has always loved the lepers. She calls them "strays," and has taught me the heart of Christ by her love. Every now and then they come around our house looking for something they never had at home. Not long ago, one young man came over holding a large, framed picture of him. His mother didn't want it anymore, so she sent it to him—along with other rejections. Kim stuck it on top of the living room cabinet—right there for everyone to see. That was statement enough: "You are accepted."

They're all around us, but conveniently hidden. Drainers. "Extra grace required." We laugh, but Christ weeps. Go with Him outside the camp (that is, join Him as an outcast). That's where the lepers are.

When Grace Reached Out to Me

When grace reached out for me,

It did not come with fanfare,

Nor break as the sun's new day.

But quietly it met me,

When I from the battle wounded lay.

Strong, nail-scarred hands embraced me,

And beckoned me to pray.

As gentle grace overwhelmed me,

And weakness fell away.

My wound—so torn—had festered,

By grace—now healed—set free!

All this and more was lifted,

When grace reached out for me.

Weep with Those Who Weep

"I don't want anything sad in the service," said the young lady whose mother had just passed away. She sat down in my office and looked at me sternly. "We won't call it a funeral; just call it a memorial service. And call the obituary a biography. This is going to be a celebration. I don't want any mourning. Is that understood?" I nodded in agreement. It had always been my practice to accommodate the desires of the family during difficult times like this. But I couldn't help but think that she was making a mistake. She seemed determined to erase all opportunity to grieve—or at least postpone the inevitable bereavement. Recognizing that a loved one has departed to be with the Lord provides tremendous consolation, but it does not replace the very real loss. In fact, to deny the loss, or cover it over with a false spirituality, can delay the healing process.

Unfortunately, it has become more and more popular today to think that we are somehow less "spiritual" if we grieve. This shallow reasoning springs from the attitude that if we have "real faith" then we won't ever have sorrow, grief, or pain. In fact, nothing could be farther from the truth.

Certainly, sorrow is temporary for the believer. And Paul said we do not sorrow as the world does, whose people have no hope. Still, sorrow remains in this broken world. Even Christ burst into tears at the weeping of those around Him, even though He knew that He was about to raise his friend Lazarus from the grave. Grieving is a natural part of a relationship, since suffering and loss are inevitable to every one.

C. S. Lewis wrote the following in one of his personal letters:

> "I have just got your letters of the 22nd containing the sad news of your father's death. But, dear lady, I hope you and your mother are not really trying to pretend it didn't happen. It does happen, happens to all of us, and I have no patience with the high-minded people who make out that it 'doesn't matter.' It matters a great deal, and very solemnly."

A friend recently asked me why God would create people if He knew that all this suffering would result. My answer was simple. We choose to have companionship and love even when we know that we will also suffer pain and loss for it. We need only look at God to see how He chose to have fellowship with us despite the excruciating pain it brought to Him.

Grief remains constant in the vicissitudes of life, but God's grace is evermore constant. He gives us hope in the midst of sorrow. May we find His grace and never think that it is unspiritual to grieve.

The Garden of His Love

I stopped along my walk to watch,
A Husbandman at work.
His slow, determined labor,
Seemed unnatural for its worth.

Against the picket fence I leaned,
To gain a closer look,
For something in the way He sowed,
Caught the glance I took.

Though many cars and people passed,
He did not seem to mind,
But methodically He worked that soil,
Planting seeds of every kind.

I watched Him press and mold each mound,
And cover every grain,
He seemed to count each kernel,
And give them tears for rain.

He whistled some old church hymn,
The name beyond recall,
Still rung within my breast and throat,
Of a distant altar call.

When He reached into His seed-bag,
I glimpsed an ugly scar,
And then my eyes were opened,
To this place I'd come so far.

Each seed was but a blessing,
From the grace of God above.
The ground His heart was working,
Was my garden of His love.

What Makes Eternity Sing?

Beat out bland ballad's vain anthem—
Life's spent breath on hedonic desire.
Nor the rhapsody upon sharp building spires—
Reaching, ever reaching for the skies.
Nor life's rapacious grasp—the overture of more.
This is not, is not, is not—
Not the everlasting score.

What makes Eternity sing?

Kind smiles—Love's melody—frail in life—
Broken as One—Scarred Exemplar!
Gives lyric to the angel's choir.

Jacob at Jabbok

Crossing Over to the Full Blessings of God

WHEN MY WIFE, Kim, and I were much younger and just beginning our ministries, we received an opportunity to serve in a new church in another state. The pastor gave us a glowing report of how the church was growing and how they needed leaders like us. In fact, he promised that we would be ordained before very long. Since I wasn't much needed in the current outreach I had helped start, this sounded like a good idea. We packed our bags and headed off cross-country. Little did we know that the pastor's glowing reports were exaggerated and that the church was actually struggling to survive.

We soon discovered that much of this new church was built on similar schemes. I believe the pastor really wanted to build a viable local church, but many of his efforts were based on his own plans, not the direction and timing of God. This pastor had tremendous insight into what people wanted and held great influence over them as a result.

Through much anguish and unfulfilled promises the church finally folded. The pastor left the state and started another church. I later learned that he had invited another couple to join him using the same kind of promises he had made to us. Eventually this church failed as well. A lot of people suffered from his schemes.

Kim and I learned a valuable, but costly, lesson about manipulation. The Kingdom of God must be built on His plans, not the schemes of humankind!

When I consider this former pastor, I am reminded of another schemer named Jacob. His story can be found in eleven chapters from Genesis 25 to 35. In chapter 32 this son of Isaac finally came face to face with God and his own sin of manipulation and wrestled with both.

You may remember that Jacob schemed to get the birthright from his twin brother Esau and connived with his mother Rebekah to gain the patriarchal blessing of Isaac. Esau declared in anguish, "Isn't he rightly named Jacob? (Jacob means "deceiver.") He has deceived me these two times: He took my birthright, and now he's taken my blessing!" That Esau would serve Jacob may have been foreordained (Ge. 25:23), but the means by which Jacob got the advantage was entirely wrong. He had taken matters into his own hands. As a result of his schemes, Esau threatened Jacob's life, and Jacob fled far away to his uncle Laban.

Not long after arriving, Jacob contrived to wrest wealth from Laban. Jacob made an agreement with his uncle to receive all the spotted or dark-colored animals as wages. Jacob thought he could make the animals have spots by pealing branches and staking them in the ground during mating season. Jacob was scheming again! But this custom had nothing to do with determining the color of sheep. Jacob's manipulations did not bring about his blessings. The only reason he was blessed was because God helped him.

Does this mean that Jacob didn't see that God was helping him? No, for he declared such to Laban (Ge. 31:3-5, 42). Nevertheless, Jacob could not come to rely solely on God. He couldn't give up control of his destiny. He kept trying to help God out. So it was with my former pastor. He tried to build a church by misleading people—giving them false hope. God may continue to bring blessing to a certain extent, but a plan built on manipulation always produces tragic results.

While Jacob was getting wealthy off his uncle, Laban's sons were getting upset at Jacob's success. Faced with their growing animosity, Jacob had no recourse but to return to Canaan. Now Jacob had Esau in front of him, whom he had cheated, and Laban's angry sons behind him. On his journey home, Jacob sent messengers to Esau to see what kind of reception he might get. They returned with alarming news: Esau was coming with four hundred men!

In great distress, Jacob schemed again. Could he somehow appease Esau? Out of desperation, he divided his flocks, herds, servants, and family into groups and sent them ahead of him as gifts to Esau. Jacob intended this series of bribes to wear down any hatred remaining in his brother (Ge. 32:22). He probably remembered the brutish nature of Esau and knew what would appeal to him—after all, Jacob had secured the birthright by appealing to Esau's hunger. Jacob was again relying on his abilities to manipulate the situation to his advantage. He still wasn't relying on God.

However, Jacob did one thing that initiated a change of heart: *he prayed*. Jacob prayed with humility, declaring, "I am unworthy of all the kindness and faithfulness you have shown your servant" (Ge. 32:10). Jacob then reminded God of His promises to bless him and bring him into the land of his fathers.

After sending the last group across the Jabbok River, Jacob was left alone with night falling. The schemer who had accumulated so much was stripped of every valuable he owned and isolated from everyone who meant anything in his life. At times like this—of complete brokenness—God often meets with us. Jacob needed a change in character and only God can affect that kind of change. Jacob had a manipulative spirit that tainted all his thinking. Only God, who wrestles with the inner man, can break such life-dominating sin.

That night, Jacob met a man at the ford who stood in his way. The two began to wrestle. (The Hebrew word for wrestle has the idea of "getting dusty"—to wrestle down in the dust and dirt.) The struggle occurred on the threshold of the Promised Land—the threshold of blessing. Jacob's manipulations had exiled him from the land of promise for years. Now God would not let him pass until he changed.

Jacob wrestled obstinately all night while the darkness concealed his adversary. "The turning point of the long bout is clear. After a long, indecisive struggle, the man 'touched' Jacob. The 'touch' was actually a blow—he dislocated his hip. But the text uses a soft term for it, demonstrating a supernatural activity."

Only when God touched Jacob's thigh and rendered him lame, did Jacob realize the awesome person of his adversary. Jacob finally faced up to his own inability. He saw his own helplessness. He had finally come to the end of himself and recognized the only source of his blessings. "When God touched the strongest sinew of Jacob, the wrestler, it shriveled, *and with it Jacob's persistent self-confidence.*" He was limping in his flesh, but he was whole in spirit! God broke Jacob's physical strength, but gave him inner solidarity.

So it is with the sin of manipulation. It can exile us from the full blessings of God for years. Eventually God makes something so difficult in our lives that we have no choice but to deal with the sin. We come to the end of ourselves and in anguish we wrestle with God. God wants to change us from being manipulative in spirit to being poor in spirit (Mt. 5:3). To be poor in spirit is to know that we need God desperately. We become poor in spirit when we recognize that God is the one who has been there all along to direct and provide and bless. He's the one in control!

Now Jacob hung on for dear life and refused to let go unless he received a blessing. Hosea says that Jacob "wept and begged for his favor" (Hos. 12:4). God blessed Jacob by changing his name (and nature) to Israel. The name "Jacob" means "heal-catcher" or usurper. What better description of his previous character! At Jabbok, however, God changed Jacob's name to Israel, which means, "he struggles with God." Jacob then named the place "Peniel," which means "face-to-face with God," because of his life-changing encounter.

When Jacob crossed over Jabbok, he faced his brother, but God gave him favor in his brother's eyes. They met and embraced and wept. Esau then asked what was the meaning of the droves sent on ahead and Jacob confessed that they were to appease Esau. But Esau had changed over the years as well and was not moved by manipulation. He told Jacob to keep the gifts.

Some of us have a Jabbok to cross but we haven't wrestled with God. We haven't come face to face with God and our own weakness. Perhaps some of us haven't really been in the blessings of God for years—exiled from His promises.

Some of us need to take the lesson from Esau and learn how *not to be* manipulated. Both are serious flaws that must be overcome. Kim and I resolved never to make a major decision unless God really confirmed it.

Are you Jacob at Jabbok, or Israel at Peniel? Are you at a place where you struggle with making your own plans work, or are you in the place of God's presence and favor? You can't enter the Promised Land as a Jacob. You must enter it as Israel with a limp. You can't manage things in your own strength, wiles, or craftiness. God will oppose you if you try. You must face Him first and wrestle till you see your utter need for Him. There has to be a whole new character change that only God can effect.

Have you crossed over to the full blessings of God? Are you Jacob at Jabbok, or Israel at Peniel?

The Accident

This skit is inspired by the picture of the girl looking at Jesus' scarred hand and asking, "Does it still hurt?"

Set: A partition at the back of the stage for actors to enter and exit or curtain stage right.

Props: Red strobe light; robe for Jesus; siren sound effect. Dry ice or a fog machine can be used to provide an ethereal, heavenly effect.

Start: Lights dim; spots on actors as they enter; a red flashing strobe light goes off behind the back partition as a siren goes off. Dry ice cloud appears.

A young father carries a daughter (who is limp in his arms) from behind the back divider. The father and daughter have grease marks and traces of blood on face and arms. The father kneels quietly on center stage. The father says, "Oh Jesus, Jesus, my little Tracy." He holds the daughter with her head in his left arm with her seated on the floor. The red light stays on but stops flashing. There is a moment where both the father and the daughter remain motionless. The daughter then gets up as the father remains kneeling with arms out as though he was still holding her. The daughter stands and looks at her father sweetly, then quietly strokes his hair. (Very quiet, "mystical" music can be played in the background.) A moment later a young woman and Jesus walk out. The daughter is not surprised and walks up to Jesus. They exchange hugs. The young woman (her mother) is on Jesus' right; the daughter is at His left.

Mother: "Is it time?"

Jesus: "Yes, in a moment."

Mother: "It was a very serious accident wasn't it?"

Jesus: "Yes, (sigh) it was terrible. Too many have died at the hands of drunk drivers."

Daughter: "He is my father, isn't he?" She turns to gaze at her father.

Jesus: "Yes, and he loves you very much." There is a slight pause and the daughter turns and looks at her mother.

Daughter: "You're my mother, aren't you? I remember you in some of Daddy's pictures."

Mother: Kneels in front of Jesus and places her hands on her daughter's shoulders. "Yes, I am your mother. I miss you and your father very much. I have been watching you all these years. I saw you give your heart to the Lord when you were five. I watched you and your father kneel and pray each night by your bed. I love you." They both hug. Jesus puts his hands on them. As they release each other Jesus takes the daughter's hands in His. The daughter notices the scars in His hands.

Daughter: "What happened to your hands?"

Jesus: "A long time ago I came to where your father is now and lived among my creation. I loved all the people so much I was willing to die for them. You see, Tracy, it was necessary for someone who has done nothing wrong to die for the sins of everyone."

Daughter: "But why are your hands scarred?"

Jesus: "My hands are scarred because my death was by crucifixion."

Daughter: "What is cru-ah-cru-fixion?"

Jesus: "Crucifixion. It is the most horrible death that can be imagined. I was stripped, beaten, and nailed to a wooden cross. To breathe, I had to drag myself up on it (demonstrates with arms outstretched) like this. And the thirst was unbearable. But most of all, my heart broke for the love of all mankind."

Daughter: Taking Jesus' hand and rubbing it, she asks, "Does it still hurt?"

Jesus: "It hurts here in my heart (Jesus places His other hand over His heart) because after all I suffered, some still do not believe."

Daughter: "Lord, I believe."

Jesus: With His hand on her head. "Yes, Tracy, I know. You gave your heart to me six months ago."

Mother: To Jesus, "Is it time?"

Jesus: Slowly, "Yes, it's time to go."

Mother and Jesus exit together. Mother turns and waves at her daughter.

The daughter waves and turns to look at her father. She walks over to him, sits down and lays in his arms again, limp.

The father now moves as though time continues. The red strobe light begins again. He brushes her hair out of her eyes. The daughter wakes and hugs him around the neck.

Daughter: "Oh, daddy!"

Father: "Oh, Tracy, Tracy, I thought I had lost you, too."

Daughter: "Daddy, Jesus came."

Father: "I'm sure He did, Tracy, I'm sure He did."

Lights fade out. Exit.

True Worship

THOSE OF US WHO ENJOYED THE MOVIE *CHARIOTS OF FIRE* remember the moment when the actor portraying the "Flying Scotsman," Eric Liddel, tilted his head back while he ran—as if raised in worship to God. Later we hear him explain, "When I run I feel his pleasure." Eric understood something about worship that we cannot miss: *worship is a life of obedience to God.*

Paul put it this way, "for it is God who works in you to will and to act according to his good purpose"—his good *pleasure* (Phil. 2:13). Worship happens when we live our lives to give him pleasure. Worship isn't just "a slow song," John Bevere once said. We tend to categorize songs as praise songs (the fast ones) and worship songs (the slow ones), but the scope of worship is far more than that. Certainly we can worship God by singing, but true worship happens in Spirit and truth. We worship God when we give him pleasure.

I feel his pleasure when I write. The words almost leap out of the depths of my being—sometimes with groaning, sometimes with joy and laughter. But it is worship. And he is working in me "to will and to act according to his good purpose."

One of the greatest privileges I have as a minister is to help families in their time of grief—when a loved one passes away. As the church gets older, we have more funerals, more memorial services to perform. It is my privilege to walk a family through that process. It demands compassion. You cannot do it just as a duty.

Sometimes I don't know the person who died, only the family. But if I do the eulogy, I always sit down with the family and they share stories about the life of the deceased. That's when love begins to work. Then I shut myself alone with God to write—not just a sermon—but a message from the person's life and the heart of God. I may not have known the deceased, but God does. In times of vulnerability, grief, and sorrow, God's compassion breaks through. That is when faith works by love. That is when I feel his pleasure.

You may sense his pleasure as you labor or serve in his kingdom. His pleasure may come as you speak with him quietly along a garden path, or give a cup of cold water to someone with great thirst. For Eric, it meant honoring God in sports, by not running on the Sabbath, teaching English to the Chinese, and dying as a missionary in war-torn China. His was a life of obedience to God. He felt his pleasure—do you?

Courage to Serve

"Courage is fear that has said its prayers."—Karl Barth

Skit

My name is Abe. No, not the "honest one." I'm the guy who started the nation of Israel—you know, the "Father of Faith." Well, let me tell you what it was like. I was minding my own business when I got this call. (Phone Rings) I pick up the phone and this voice says, "Abe?" I said, "Yah, it ain't Joe's Pool Hall."
This voice says, "Abe, start packing."
I said, "Packing? Is this my mother-in-law in a disguised voice?"
He says, "Abe, I want you to leave your relatives and your country."
I said, "Now I know this is my mother-in-law."
He said, "Abe, this is God. Start packing."
Talk about a direct line.
So I said, "Is this the IRS?"
After a moment of silence He said, "Not that god. I'm the one that has mercy."
"Ohhh, that one. Tell me then, where am I going?"
"To the land I will show you."
"Riigghhtt!" So I hang up. No way am I leaving my comfort zone. Nobody is going to tell me where to go.
(Phone Rings Again – twice or three times)

"Hello."

"Abe!"

"Whhaatt!"

"This is God. Start packing."

"OK, let's just say I believe you. What do I get out of this?"

"Blessings."

"Blessings? I'm going to leave everything to follow who knows what to who knows where, just for blessings? What kind of blessings?"

"You will have progeny."

"Just a minute. Hey Sarah, what's progeny? I'm going to have what? Look, I'm seventy-five years old! You call this a blessing?"

"Abe!"

"Whhaatt!"

"Start packing."

Every one of us should be packing something. By that I mean that we should be preparing for service. Getting ready. Our packing might be in the form of education, service to our church or community, or developing our devotional life. Sometimes God will literally tell us to start packing—to get ready for a change. He may call us to local ministry, or He may call us to distant places. In any case, we should be preparing. Whatever our gifts are, we should develop them.

It takes courage to break out of our comfort zones and take a risk to follow Him. Let me give you a recent example. The children around

Rose-a-lie Stewart's housing complex didn't have any supervision and were getting into trouble. She volunteered to help with the children and started having Bible studies and activities with them. When I called to ask if she would teach a class on Sundays, she jumped at the chance. God had seen her faithfulness. She may even be able to use some of our resources to help the children in her community.

When God called Kim and me over twenty years ago, we traveled from Alaska to Colorado to Florida. We moved about eight times in two years to try to help four different churches get started. When we arrived in Florida, I think we had less than a dollar between us. Now, when we look back, some of those churches are doing well and some of them did not continue. But all of that ministry was preparation for the future. What is courage?

1. *Courage is the willingness to take a risk,* just like Abraham who didn't know where he was going.

> By faith Abraham, when called to go to a place he would later receive as his inheritance, obeyed and went, even though he did not know where he was going. By faith he made his home in the promised land like a stranger in a foreign country; he lived in tents, as did Isaac and Jacob, who were heirs with him of the same promise. For he was looking forward to the city with foundations, whose architect and builder is God.—He. 11:8-10

2. *Courage stands on convictions in the face of criticism and challenge.* Courage comes in the form of Mother Teresa's nurses who "tenderly dab the sores of lepers and cradle the sick until death." Sometimes even Mother Teresa was criticized: "Why care for those who are doomed anyway?" But she explained, "They are created by God; they deserve to die with dignity." (And in doing this, she ministered to Christ (Mt. 25:40).) Not only is this great compassion, but this is

great courage—facing disease, stench, and death with little or no earthly reward.

Lack of courage is to choose safety for oneself at the expense of others. Pilate was merciful until it became too risky. It takes great courage to stand alone (Ex. 23:2). But God's blessings follow those who are courageous.

What are you packing? What has God called you to do?

If You and I Were Snowflakes

A Bedtime Poem for My Daughters
Cathy, Tamara, Rachel, Deborah, and Lora

If you were a snowflake,

Far up in the sky,

You'd lay your head on pillow clouds,

And sleep near angels proud.

If you were a snowflake,

Drifting in the sky,

You'd dream of trees and mountain peeks,

That tickle your fluffy sheets.

If I was a snowflake,

Sent from heaven above,

I'd light upon a little girl's cheek,

And kiss her smile so sweet.

Goodnight!

The Carnival Box

Chapter 1

Mom says that going to the carnival makes her as "'cited as a bug in a tater patch." I guess that goes for me, too. The smell of popcorn and cotton candy and riding the roller coaster must be like heaven.

"How's my nine-year-old birthday boy?"

I just smiled. Mom sure was pretty. We may not have much, but all the boys at school told me she was "shore somethin' ta look at."

"It's getting' late an' I don't have any more money to spend," she said as she bent over and ran her fingers through my hair. "I'm already short on rent. You know how Myrtle is about being late on the payments. But it's yer birthday, an' she'll just have to accept it. 'Sides, she can't throw us out, who'll rent that ol' dump. Here's one last ticket. Now go have some fun."

One last ticket, I thought. *I'd have to make it count. I walked alongside the Tilt-O-Whirl and up to the game booths. Maybe I could win something for mom.* Just as I was pondering what to do, something supernatural got hold of me—I could tell because those chills went down my spine—you know, the kind you get at church when the preacher's sweating and almost singing and everyone's amen'in.

Just then the wind took the ticket right out of my hands. It sailed end-over-end to the game booths, with me right after it. That ticket blew under a crowd and I was on my hands and knees to find it, squirming through the legs and long dresses (some lady yelped). I chased it right up to the edge of a booth. When I grabbed it, I pushed my way up to get some air and see where I was. I had arrived at the ring-toss booth (and everyone was scowling at me). So I put my elbows and chin on the counter to watch. One of the High School lettermen was trying to impress his girl. But each ring he tossed bounced around and fell to the table missing its mark.

"Ah, great try!" announced the old man behind the counter (who, like me, was not much taller than the top of the counter). "You've got a gr-r-r-reat throwing arm," he said, his voice trailing off like Tony the Tiger. "But this is all in the wrist—all in the wrist. Who else would like to try? Ring a bottle and take home one of these cute, cuddly Koala bears! Just one ticket gets you three tries."

"Mister, I want to," I found myself saying, holding out my ticket.

"Well, what have we here," said the old man. "Someone I can see eye-to-eye. You came to the right place. Here are three rings. You can try for these easy bottles up front and win a Koala, or you can try for the big

bottle in back and choose any prize in this booth."

I gazed at all the toys and stuffed animals as I picked up the bamboo

rings. They felt so light I thought they might rise right out of my hands.

I was about to take aim when Horace slid up beside me. Horace was the

bully in class, *and Myrtle's son*. (Mom always said Horace was "as ugly

as homemade sin.") Horace spit out the grass blade he was chewing and

smiled a fat, sly grin at me.

"Ya thain't gonna throw them, am ya?" he said with a slight hissing

sound through a missing tooth.

"Might could," I said weakly.

"My mom thes this here's a thissy game. Nobody wins this. Bet ya

can't ring one."

"Bet so."

"Prove it."

I flipped the first one and it sailed between two bottles.

"Ha! Clean miss. Ya ain't good 'thall."

"Am so."

"Prove it."

I took aim with the second ring and let it go. It ricocheted off the top of

a bottle and bounced to the table.

"There. Yer a loother."

I didn't say anything this time and just took aim. I don't know if Horace thought I might ring the last one or what, but just as I tossed the ring, he kicked me so hard my feet left the ground. The ring seemed to sail in slow motion up to the tent top, clattered against the rafters, and fell back down on top of the large bottle in back. With my jaw hanging down, I watched it spin around the bottle like a top and fall over the neck. Everyone gasped.

"A winner!" announced the little man. "We have a winner!"

"Thissy," muttered Horace as he left with a shove.

My sore rump was glad to see him go. I rubbed it gently.

"The young lad has a ringer on *the-e-e* biggest bottle," continued the little man. "Take your pick young man. What will it be? A Koala bear or one of these bright red fire engines—or maybe one of our MYSTERY boxes? It could contain a million dollars or a monkey's paw for wishes. Or maybe it hides a surprise—something everyone needs."

I studied the many toys and exotic-looking things to choose from—then remembered to get something for mom. "I want that one, Mister." The box I pointed to was about the size of a lunch pail and brightly decorated. Mom liked colorful things. This box would be perfect for her mantle.

"Ah, that box is special. *Very* special. Are you sure you want that one? For some it's a Pandora's box; but for some, and only some mind you, it's a treasure chest."

"It's for my mom."

"Not for you?" quizzed the little man with a smile. "In that case, it's the perfect one. The greatest treasures are the ones we give away." I thought I caught a gleam in the little man's eye.

He used a stool to pull the box down, blew some dust off it, and put it on the counter.

"They say this came from Poland. See that bear driving the sleigh? I think he was trying to get away from the box." The little man laughed from his belly. "You'll like this box, son. I guarantee it."

I took the box in both hands, pushed my way back through the crowd, and ran to the nearest bench. Holding it felt like Christmas—or maybe like I had just gotten an "A" on a spelling test—or won a race in gym class—maybe all rolled into one. I rubbed the lacquered finish. It was a fine wood box. Mom would like it. I shook it and didn't hear anything rattle. The lid was stuck, but I managed to pop it off. A pleasant odor came out—like sweet flowers or something. Just then mom found me.

"Ready to go?" she asked with her hands on her hips. (She always put her hands on her hips when she was in a hurry.)

"Yah. Look what I won. It's for you." I slid the lid back on and held it up.

"Oh, Honey. For me? How wonderful." She took the box and eyed it closely. "It's so-o-o-o..." Mom hesitated, then decided on "pretty."

"Thank you so much," she said as she gave me a big squeeze. "Come along now. We need to get on home."

Getting home meant riding in our '54 Pontiac—the kind that had the stick shift on the steering column. It was big and sky blue. You couldn't miss it with all the slimmer fin-tailed cars in the lot.

Mom set the box down next to me as we climbed in. She started chatting about Myrtle and the house and work and stuff, but I just looked at the box. That sure was a funny bear on it. I wondered if something was really in it. I slipped off the lid again and peered inside. Something small and white was at the bottom. I turned the box over and shook out a card into my lap. On the card were these words: "Desires of the heart fill the prayers of the soul." I whispered the words softly and rubbed the gold-embossed letters. That same chill tingled up my spine. Just then I heard mom complain.

"Myrtle's going to be angry. I wish I had fifty more dollars."

"I wish you did too, mom."

As we drove away, I put the card into my wallet and closed the box. Looking back, the lights of the carnival twinkled softly like fireflies on a hot July night.

Chapter 2

"Hello-e-e-e."

That was Myrtle sticking her head in the front door. (Mom says she squeaks like a rain frog.) Myrtle was always late—except when it came to collecting the rent. Then she was right on time: seven Sunday morning sharp. We were still upstairs getting ready for church. (Mom said she always wondered what the good Lord had against us to send her on the Sabbath.)

"It's Myr-tle. Ren-ty time," she called out in her singsong voice.
I peeked down from between two posts in the banister, but mom came to the top of the stairs—with her hands on her hips.
"I'll be right there, Myrtle," she said, "Make yourself at home." *Doesn't that lady ever knock?* she fussed under her breath.
I watched as Myrtle came in with Horace in tow. Myrtle was short and hen-plump. Horace was always polite around Myrtle. He caught a glimpse of me and smiled real big. I ducked.
Mom went back to primping her hair in the hall mirror. "Now Myrtle," she called out, "I don't want you to get upset or nothin'. Things have been right tight this month—with the mill closin' n all. All I got's in the box on the mantle. You're welcome to it. I'll have the rest as soon as I start down at the Pit."

The "Pit" was the local truck stop and Bar-B-Q. They had the best pig in town. Mom was going to waitress there first thing Monday. She had a good job at the mill, but times were hard in the fabric business and they had a big lay off.

I watched as Myrtle marched on her heals over to the fireplace. But instead of grabbing the moneybox, she took hold of the box I won at the fair. Before I could object, she popped the lid off and shook a greenback into her hand.

"E-e-e-e-e!" she shrieked. "Look it here. You sure are one to pull my leg. This must be a brand new fifty-dollar bill!"

Mom went to the top of the stairs again. "What do you mean?"

"Why, the rent of course!" Myrtle fluttered the fifty-dollar bill over her head.

"But I didn't..."

"Don't look so awful fuzzed up. I knew I could count on you to make the rent. Thanky, I gotta run." Myrtle set the box back on the mantel and ushered Horace out the door.

(*Gone to torture some other renters*, I thought.)

Mom scurried down the stairs with me right behind her. She picked up the box and eyed it carefully. She then gave me a puzzled stare.

"I don't know where it came from, honest," I said, sheepishly. "It wasn't there last night."

Mom slid the lid back on the box and looked out the window after

Myrtle. "Well, doesn't that take the huckleberry off the bush."

Chapter 3

It was hard sitting on wood pews and waiting for the preaching to end—

especially with the sun shinning through the windows and beckoning my

thoughts outside—it was simply "outdacious."

I got the fidgets and started playing with my wallet. Everyone knew the

service was just about to end because Thelma Lou was called up front to

sing "Amazing Grace." (Thelma Lou was the mayor's wife and always

sang at the end—except that time last winter when she had the croup.

Everyone still talks about what a wonderful service that was. They say

Thelma Lou once trained to be an opera singer, but her voice broke from

over training. She never recovered. Mom says it must be for penance

that we had to hear her sing. I wasn't too sure what penance was, but I

wondered if God ever covered His ears.)

As Thelma Lou hit the "there" of "When we've been there 10,000

years," she squawked and I dropped my wallet. A few coins and my

baseball cards spilled out. Among them was the card from mom's box.

Mom shushed me and I scooped up my belongings. Then she patted my

knee and whispered, "I wish she could sing better, don't you?"

When she said that, the thought crossed my mind for the first time—one of those crazy, kid's world, impossible thoughts. I rubbed the card again and whispered, "me too." Before the words left my mouth, Thelma Lou suddenly crooned the purest, sweetest note I ever heard. At that moment, I think everyone in the room held their breath. Even the flies stopped buzzing. Thelma Lou held her hand over her mouth and gave a dumbfounded look at the organist (who had her hands frozen in midair). You should have seen the bug-eyed look on the preacher's face. Thelma Lou composed herself and cleared her throat. The organist started again. What came out was the grandest thing ever heard in that little, country church. When she finished, everyone stood and applauded and cheered—right there in the service. Mom said it was a genuine miracle.

When we got home I looked at the box on the mantle. Somehow the lid had popped off and was lying on the floor. I slid it back on and wondered.

Chapter 4

Since Mom was working the noon-to-nine shift at the Pit, we were sleeping in a tad. A knock at the front door sent me in pajamas to see who was there. A state trooper smiled when I peeked through the front window. I opened the door a crack.

"Hey son! Your mom at home?" he said.

I shut the door and yelled upstairs. "Mom!"

"Tell them to come back later," was the weak reply.

"Mom! There's a state trooper at the door."

I heard a thump, then mom appeared in her bathrobe at the top of the stairs.

"What? Who?"

"There's a state trooper at the door," I repeated.

"Well, don't be rude, let him in."

I opened the door again and said in my most polite voice, "Come on in, sir."

The trooper took his hat and sunglasses off as mom came down the stairs. He looked strong and handsome—the kind of guy you'd like to have as a big brother. When mom looked at him she almost forgot the last step—and tripped forward. Only a quick catch by the trooper saved her from spilling flat on the floor. I don't think I had seen mom so red.

"Are you alright, ma-am?"

"Yes. Thank you," she stuttered. "So clumsy of me." Mom brushed her robe down.

"Sorry to disturb you, ma'am, my name is Trooper Reyes."

"I'm Ruby Brown and this is my son, Thomas."

"One of the neighbors had their car stolen last night," he said, "and we're just asking the neighbors if they heard anything unusual."

Mom shook her head. "Nothin' I recollect." She looked at me and I shook my head.

"Well, it's a red Oldsmobile Starfire convertible—a real one-of-a-kind beauty. If you see or hear anything please call us at the station."

"We'll keep an eye out," said mom.

As the trooper turned to go, he caught sight of the box on the mantle and stopped abruptly. "Where did you get that box, if you don't mind me asking?"

"My son won it at the carnival."

"May I?" he asked.

"Sure go ahead."

The trooper picked it up as though he had found a treasure. "My grandparents were immigrants from Poland and had a box just like this one. I used to keep some, well, some of my favorite things in it. Don't know what happened to it, though." Sliding it back on the mantle, he sighed, "Sorry to bother you, ma'am. I better go make my report. Let me know if you hear anything."

Mom closed the door slowly while her eyes followed the trooper all the way out to his patrol car. When she tried to take a step back, she realized her bathrobe was caught in the door.

I crossed my arms at her and scolded, "Mom!"

"What?" she said in denial. (But I saw a sheepish grin.)

I rode with mom down to the Pit. I was supposed to hang out at the

fountain and then visit Aunt Flossie. All the while I had a bad feeling—

like something odd was about to happen. I didn't know until later, but

Horace let himself into our place. I think he wanted to see if there was

any more money in the carnival box. He took it and slipped out the back,

making toward the woods along the old dirt road. (You had to be careful

down that road because Old Man Twitter lived along it. They say he

kept his window propped open with a small block of wood. That way he

could shoot unlucky squirrels and anything else that moved. Mom says

some lady visiting from the city had a little white dog get loose back

there. Old Man Twitter cured it of yapping.)

When Horace got far enough from the house, he sat down on a stump

and started to pry the lid off the box. All it took was a crack. Horace let

out a yelp, dropped the box, and held his nose. The odor from the box

was something like Limburger cheese, polecat, and that stink when

something dies under your porch. Horace gave the box a kick and it

landed next to the road. But that didn't help, the smell was all over his

hands—and stayed there for a week. Horace lit out for home, taking the

shorter path through Old Man Twitter's yard. He got nicked in the rump for his trespass. When he got home, they had to burn his clothes and tried a concoction of lemon oil, lye, and molasses on his hands, but nothing would take out the smell. When he tried to go to midweek service, we all lined up in the hall holding our noses. The pastor sent him home. Myrtle made him stay out with the chickens.

I heard from one of the farmers that while the box lay beside the road, a red convertible full of young sharecroppers drove by it, skidded to a stop, and then slowly backed up. The side door opened and one hand reached out to grab the half-opened box. Just as the car started forward, the doors exploded open and four young teens jumped out—two over the back. As the car ran aimlessly into the ditch, they all stood and watched a large snake slither out and go beneath the car. Seeing the car stuck and not wanting to get close to its guardian, they chided each other for their bad luck and decided to leave on foot. I don't know if the story was true, but the state troopers did find the abandoned vehicle.

When we got home, Trooper Reyes was waiting for us with the box. "Evening, ma'am." He tipped his hat. "I wonder if I could ask you some questions."

"Certainly, officer. Won't you come in?" Mom's voice sounded a bit concerned. She must have wondered, like me, what the officer was doing with the box. We stepped into the foyer and mom was the first to ask, "Did you find the stolen car?"

"Yes, ma'am."

"Please call me Ruby," interrupted mom.

"Yes, well Ruby, ma'am, we found the car an hour or so ago," said the trooper. "It was abandoned down by the old road." He held the box up. "And this was found in it."

"The box?" mom exclaimed with a surprised look. My jaw dropped.

"How did it…" her voice trailed off.

"We thought you might be able to explain that to us," said the trooper.

"I don't know," said mom. "I haven't seen it since you were here this morning. I went to work with my son and haven't been back till now."

"Where do you work?" he asked.

"Down at the Dwyer Bar-B-Q," mom replied, with her hands on her hips again.

The officer looked at me. "And where was your son today?"

"I dropped him off at the drug store. He was to visit his aunt today." Mom scowled at me.

"I don't know anything, honest," I pleaded. "I had a soda and then went straight to Aunt Flossie's."

The trooper looked at both of us and then smiled. "I believe you, but we have to check any leads," he said. "I'll have to keep the box for a while—until we settle this. Thank you for your trouble, ma'am."

"Thank you," said mom with a sigh, and let the trooper out.

"That box has been one powerful strange thing," mom said as she shut the door.

Chapter 5

After making his rounds the next day, Trooper Reyes sat down at his desk and shuffled some of his paperwork. His chief came over.

"Get any leads on that stolen car?" his chief asked.

"Not a thing," Trooper Reyes admitted. "Everything checked out. It baffles me how that box got in the car. Maybe whoever stole the car, stole it later." He picked the box up again and began to rub some scratches on it.

"Well, at least we got the car back in one piece," said the chief. "Nice car, huh?"

"Yah, nice car. What I don't understand is why there would be footprints on the back trunk."

"Yup. That's an odd one."

Trooper Reyes remembered that the box was open in the convertible, but he felt like he should open it again. He slipped his fingers under the lid and popped it off. The lid almost jumped in his hands and he fumbled to catch it. Peering inside, he found the box empty again. "Odd," he muttered.

Then he suddenly felt an insatiable desire for some coffee and banana-cream pie.

"Think I'll take lunch," he said as he stood up and grabbed his hat. "Are we done with this box, chief?"

"Sure. You can return it."

"Do they serve banana-cream pie down at the Dwyer pit?"

"Yup, best in the county."

"That's where I'm headed," he said as he flew out the door with the box under his arm.

You could smell the open pit Bar-B-Q miles away. It held some kind of irresistible siren song over any truckers who happened by. Mom says those at the counter stools looked like a bunch of potatoes on Popsicle sticks. She was busy taking an order when Trooper Reyes slid up to the counter. He was eyeing the pies in the glass display, but soon caught her looking at him. He *didn't* notice the small man seated next to him. Mom walked up. "Coffee?"

"Thanks, please, and I'll have a large piece of pie—banana cream," Trooper Reyes replied, smiling. He took his hat off and set it on the counter with the box.

"Good choice," came the comment from the small man seated next to him. "Excellent pie," he added, patting his belly and burping slightly. "That's a fine box you have there. May I see it?"

Trooper Reyes eyed the little man. "It's not my box, it belongs to the young lady behind the counter. You'll need to ask her."

"Well—sure, it was a prize my son won for me at the carnival" said mom, as she poured a cup of coffee for the trooper.

The short, old man carefully picked up the box and rubbed it softly. Trooper Reyes couldn't help but notice. "Have we met?" he asked. "You look vaguely familiar."

"Excuse my manners, I am Mr. Fulgari." He shook Trooper Reyes' hand vigorously. "This box is from the Gypsies of Poland. I should know. I have traveled with them many times."

"You are from Poland?" asked Trooper Reyes. "My grandparents were Polish, too."

"Yes," said Mr. Fulgari, "I can see it in your face. It is quite amazing that you should have this box, too. Among Gypsies, it is a traditional wedding gift—a box of wishes. I should know. I have made many wedding matches."

Mom caught a glance from Trooper Reyes and blushed.

"But I have no more boxes—and no more matches to make," said Mr. Fulgari with a sigh. With that, the little man popped the lid off the box. "What a wonderful aroma," he said. "Must be the smell of love." With that, the little man laid the box and some change on the counter and left.

Mom was getting off her shift soon, so Trooper Reyes ordered another piece of pie. Minutes later, he offered to walk her out to the car. Outside they looked at the old stone bridge and decided to detour for a longer walk. On the bridge, they stopped to watch the river rush below. Mom set the box on the bridge rail.

"He was an odd little man, wasn't he?" asked Trooper Reyes.

"Oh, yes, he was. But very nice." She paused a moment. "You know," said mom slowly, "I don't even know your first name."

"It's Robert. But please call me Bob."

As Bob and my mom walked on along the bank below the bridge, four young men crept out of the woods looking for some adventure.

"Let's grab another set of wheels," said one.

"Yeah, I don't like all this walking," said another.

"There's a barbeque on the other side of the bridge. Come on."

As the boys started to cross the bridge they saw the carnival box on the rail—and stopped short. They all gasped, "No. It can't be."

"This must be a sign from God," whispered the youngest.

"Gimmie a stick," said the leader, "Let's see if there's another snake in it." While he poked the box, the others backed slowly away. All of a sudden, it seemed to leap into the river. The boys screamed and scattered.

(I know all this 'cause my step dad told me a jail bird confessed to it.)

"Oh no!" Bob exclaimed, running to the bank as he caught sight of the box. It floated down the river and out of sight.

Mom took his hand and squeezed it. "It's alright," she said. "It seemed to cause a lot of trouble, but it I think it answered my wish."

"What do you mean?" Bob replied. All he got was a smile. "That deserves a kiss," he said.

Not far downstream, a little man was fishing by himself—but his catch wasn't of the finned variety. "So you thought you didn't have it in you anymore," he said to himself, as he pulled the box into a net. "You're the best! The Boss will be happy with this one."

Next Sunday, Trooper Reyes escorted mom and I to church. The place was packed because everyone in the county had heard about the crooning of Thelma Lou.

I felt sad about losing the box, but somehow things seemed the way they should.

Mom must have seen my disappointment. She leaned over and ran her fingers through my hair. "Know what I think?" she whispered. "God looks out for us."

I just smiled. (I liked what mom had to say.)

The Mist and the Sand

A Fairy Tale

Chapter 1

When spring finally breaks its hold on the long winter months in the northern kingdoms, the land and its creatures rejoice. But not for the men of two kingdoms—for spring is also the time when kings go out to war. These two kingdoms clashed in a perennial struggle for so many years that few could remember the reasons for it. Each year the people cheered their armies marching out to battle. And each year they watched them return—weary and haggard, carrying their wounded and dead with them.

When Princess Nora of the eastern realm first held her father's hand on the castle balcony to wave the troops off to battle, she thought how grand it must be to march off to war. But when she grew of age, she saw for the first time the carts return with the wounded, dead and dying on them. She ran through the castle corridors and opened its tall, broad doors to gaze in horror at the bloodied men as they slowly passed by. The king found her and gathered her in his embrace and closed the doors behind them. In tears she vowed to herself that she must someday put an end to this.

In time the princess discovered the nurse's corps, and, over the king's objections, donned their garments and followed the men off to war. On the field of battle she gained the reputation as an angel of kindness for she gave the wounded bread and water, and dressed their wounds— fearlessly braving the battle around her. She cared for all the soldiers— those of her kingdom and those who opposed them. It made no difference to her. But none knew her real name except the royal household.

One day, as the battle grew fierce in front of her, the princess and her company of nurses waited for things to clear before they could begin their work. Soon, the cries of the wounded overwhelmed her fears. Despite the pleas of the other nurses, she grabbed her bag and ran off to the front. "Wait here until the battle quiets," she called to the others— and disappeared into the woods and smoke.

It was only moments until she came upon a clearing in the battlefield. As the smoke lifted, she froze in shock. All around her lay the dead and dying. She had not seen such a killing field in all her time in the nurse's corps. For a moment, she did not even know where to begin. Then a moan close to her caught her attention and she jumped to work. She dressed one wound after another—bandages and tourniquets and water flowed from her graceful hands. Soon her apron was stained with blood. Her heart was broken, but there was no time for tears.

As she finished giving a young soldier a drink, she considered whether she would soon have to return for more supplies. Rising from a wounded soldier, she turned to see a strange man standing behind her. Her heart jumped. "Sir, you startled me! I did not hear you behind me."

The man wore a dark robe with a hood—almost like a priest—and leaned upon a staff. "You are the princess of the Eastern realms?" the man asked in a tone almost more of a command than a question.

The princess was taken aback. She knew what the risk might be if the enemy learned who she was and captured her. Glancing about, she took a breath of courage and spoke quickly, "I am, but these men must not know. Now please let me continue my work."

The man grasped her arm. "I need bread to eat and water to drink."

"Sir, what little I have must be given to these wounded you see all around you. Their need is so great."

"I have not eaten in several days," said the man. "Will you take compassion on a feeble soul?"

The princess looked closer at the pale man, and without hesitation, reached into her bag. "All I have left is this small loaf and a bit of water. But I will return with more. There is much more to do here."

The man took the bread and canteen from the princess' bloodied hands.

"Your father's pride helped cause the toll you see here today."

"My father?"

"Yes. But I have found your heart does not follow his." The man turned and disappeared in a flame before her. The light was so bright that the princess could barely see when she opened her eyes. As she groped about her, a distant voice proclaimed, "Beware the mist and the sand."

Chapter 2

Prince Frederick of the western kingdom prided himself on his generalship. He never felt prouder than leading the troops out the castle gates under his father's salute. The prince's strategy each year was to put an end to the eastern kingdom once and for all. He would show everyone how great a general he really was. As he spun his steed toward the valleys, he determined in his heart that this would be the final year—the year of victory!

The battle raged for weeks with neither side gaining the upper hand—until a lieutenant rode into the camp with news from the front. The right flank of the enemy was weakened by the last assault and if the general gave the order to press the attack, he believed the enemy could be routed from the field. Unfortunately, it would be dusk soon and the opportunity would be lost. The prince ordered his steed to be prepared. He would personally oversee the attack.

The officers and guard set off down the narrow road to the front with the prince leading the troop. There was the sound of cannon in the distance.

Suddenly, rounding the bend in the road, the general pulled hard on his reigns, nearly striking a man standing in the middle of the road. The guards quickly surrounded him. But the man looked unfazed. He stooped somewhat over a walking stick in his hands. The general signaled the guards to lower their pistols.

"Old man," he said. "You were almost run down by my steed. You should be more careful, especially with the battle so near. Be off now—before my guards drive you off the road!"

The old man looked the prince carefully in the eyes. "I am tired and I've come a long way to see the prince of the western kingdom."

The prince sneered. "I am the prince. And now you have found me. Out of my way!"

The old man stood his ground. "I have seen the battle and have come to test you. I am tired and I've come a long way. All I ask for is a little water and some bread for my journey and I'll be on my way."

"We have nothing to spare," lied the prince, as he moved his steed to go around the old man. (He had supplies, of course, but was now in a great hurry. He had no time for this delay; it could cost him the battle.)

The old man grabbed the reigns of the prince's horse in his hand and raised his stick. "Because you had only the battle in your heart and no compassion to provide my simple request, now hear my words. For the next twelve days—if you survive that long—when you touch food, it will

turn to sand, and when you take drink, it will turn to mist. Only if
another offers it to you can you receive sustenance. But if anyone offers
to give you food or drink, that person will take this curse from you upon
them forever."

The prince drew his sword to drive the man away from his steed, but as
he raised the sword to strike, the old man disappeared in a flame. He
was gone in a moment before their eyes! The prince's horse reared up
from the flame and protected the prince from the blinding light.

As the prince steadied his steed, he could see the look of horror in the
guard's faces. But his thoughts soon turned to the battle. "Quickly!" he
said. "We have no time to lose."

It was dusk when they reached the front. The prince dismounted and
entered the officer's tent to everyone's salutes. "Give me an update," he
commanded. The officers rolled out a map showing the battle front.

"We will strike now," said the prince pointing to his troops. "Here at the
flank."

"The men are exhausted," objected one of the officers.

"I don't care," snapped the prince, irritated by all the delays. "We will
end this now!"

At that moment a messenger arrived, saluted and handed the prince his
dispatch. It was from the front. The enemy was reinforcing the weak

flank. "Too late!" thought the prince. "That old man has snatched away my victory." He wadded the dispatch and threw it to the ground.

"Out! Out! Everyone out! Now!" the prince roared and threw the map off the table. The officers all departed with a brief salute. The prince leaned on the table and closed his eyes. The emotions of failure flooded up from deep within—and a gnawing regret that he could not end this war. He was angry, but he didn't want his generals to see that he really despised this endless struggle. And above all that, he felt lonely, so lonely here. His eyes began to fill with tears.

"Sir," interrupted the camp's cook. "I've brought you some food." The prince quickly brushed away the tears. The cook set the tray on the table, and, feeling that he had made the prince uncomfortable, stepped out, pulling the tent flaps shut behind him.

For a moment, everything seemed very still. The prince was quiet— fighting a large lump swelling again in his throat. *If I had only arrived a few minutes sooner...*, he thought. *I should have run that man over! What did that crazy fool say—bread and water turned to sand and mist? I shouldn't have hesitated to raise my sword against him!*

The prince reached for the bread and cheese on the plate—then stopped. *What if...? Nonsense!* He took a piece and quickly tossed it into his mouth. The next moment, he was spitting out lumps and bits of sand.

"What has that cook done?" he roared, almost gagging as he shouted.

Turning to the tent door he stepped outside, still spitting sand. The soldiers outside the tent turned and stared. "Are you alright, sir?" One of the officers asked. "Get me something to drink" said the prince. "I think the cook has tried to kill me!"

Still not believing what had happened to him, the prince grabbed a tin cup from an officer beside him and pressed it to his lips to take a drink. To his horror, all he received was a face full of mist. "What? No!" he shouted, throwing the cup to the ground. "This cannot be—food and water are now sand and mist!"

The guards who had ridden with him looked at each other and exclaimed (almost in unison), "It's the curse!" They slowly backed away from the prince.

At that moment an artillery shell exploded at the edge of the camp—scattering everyone for shelter. Another shell exploded near the prince, sending him sprawling into a ditch where he struck his head on a log and passed out.

When the prince came to, he awoke to darkness and the smell of smoke. He moaned a little as he rubbed his sore head. Pulling himself to his feet, he took a few woozy steps out of the ditch. Several calls of "Hello!" brought no response. Still disoriented, the prince struggled forward, but soon lost his way in the woods. Coming to a brook, he knelt to dip his hand in to splash water on the wound on his head. Reaching again to take a drink, the water swirled to a mist just as it touched his lips. "No!" he groaned and tried again to drink—to no avail. He sat back and sighed. He was getting thirsty now and wondered how he would get back to his lines. Everything looked unfamiliar—and he had the sinking feeling that he was also lost.

Struggling again to his feet, he decided to follow the stream to see where it led. "Twelve days like this?" he muttered to himself.

Prince Frederick walked along the stream deeper into the forest. Gathering storm clouds made it difficult to see where he was going, but he soon stepped into a large clearing. As he worked his way forward, he nearly tripped over the body of a dead soldier. It was one of his men! Backing away, he tripped over another body. He realized now that he was on the edge of a great battlefield. Glancing about, he began to make out the shapes of bodies lying all around.

Chapter 3

"Who's there?" came a voice just near a rocky knoll. "Is someone there?" It was a woman's voice.

What could a woman be doing here? The prince thought. "I'm a soldier, I've lost my way," said the prince.

"Well, I'm a nurse—but a bright light left me almost blind. I need to find my way back to the nurse's wagon. Can you help me?"

"I'm not sure," was all the prince could muster.

Just as the prince spoke, the sky erupted with lightning. The thunder let them know it was close.

"Rain is coming soon," said the nurse. "There isn't time to find the wagon. I'm not really sure they are still near us, anyway. I should have heard from them by now. However, there is an old cabin not far from here. If you can be my eyes, I can show you where to go to find shelter. However, there are several wounded here. They will need to be carried to the house as well."

"I will take you," said the prince.

A torrent of rain began to fall.

As the nurse told him where to find the cabin, the prince noticed the nurse was young and very slender. He figured she was of the eastern realm since his own kingdom had no such nurse's corps. But he also knew their reputation for helping *all* the troops. He decided to do what he could to assist her.

The prince picked up one of the wounded men to carry to the cabin. Taking hold of the prince's arm, the princess noticed his strength. *He is well built, and he must be a tall soldier*, she thought. They soon found the old cabin just on the edge of the clearing.

"Now quickly," said the nurse, "gather the rest of the wounded and bring them here. There were at least two more next to where I sat." She touched him gently on the arm as she spoke. The prince was not accustomed to this, and it struck him that the nurse was totally at his mercy. Other, less honorable men would have taken advantage of her.

The prince ran back to the clearing and found the men. He gathered each one in his arms and brought them, one by one, into the cabin. He laid them carefully on the floor in front of the fireplace, and then broke up some old chairs to start a fire. Through the light of the fire, the prince noticed that one soldier was from the western realm and two were his soldiers. He also noticed the blood stains on the nurse's clothes.

The nurse found the men and felt their foreheads. They were barely conscious. "They are not well," she whispered. "They need fresh water."

"I think there is a rain barrel outside," said the prince. "Let me see if there is a something we can use to gather some water."

"Thank you," said the princess, "you were a godsend. But, please, you will need to dry off soon, yourself. There's been enough suffering today. I don't need someone sick to take care of—especially when I can barely see."

The prince stared at her for a moment, then dug around the cabin and picked up an old tin cup on a shelf. As he did he thought about his own thirst. "Mist and sand," he mumbled.

"What did you say?" said the princess, recalling the warning from the strange man.

"Nothing," said the prince. "Let me get the water."

After returning with the cup full, he found the princess on the floor leaning against the wall fast asleep—exhausted. The prince sat next to the fire to try to dry out a little. It seemed to bring an enchanting calm and warmth to the leaky cabin. He looked at the wounded for a moment. They were bandaged neatly, but looked pale. Waking each of them gently one by one, he took the cup and gave each one a drink. When he was done, he looked at the sip left in the bottom of the cup. Lifting it to his lips, the water disappeared in a mist. *No use*, he thought, *in just a few days I will be dead from lack of water.* Placing the remaining wood on the fire, he lay down. *At least my last deeds will be honorable,* he thought.

The rain continued into the prince's dreams where he imagined drinking from a large fountain and eating at one of his father's large banquet tables. The morning broke gray and rainy with only smoke coming from the fire.

The door creaked open slowly as two men surveyed the room.

"Wounded soldiers," one muttered. "And a nurse!" nudged the other.

They stooped over the nurse and one reached out to squeeze her cheek.

"What have we here?" he said.

Chapter 4

Princess Nora awoke with a start to find two rough men looking down on her. One of them grabbed her hair and pulled her to one side. Nora yelped and grabbed the hand holding her.

All of a sudden, one of the men went flying against the wall. The other turned just in time to find a fist landing on his jaw, the force of which sent him sprawling to the floor. Both saw they were facing an officer of the western realm who drew his sword and pointed it at them.

"You have to the count of five to leave these premises," the prince barked. "One, two…"

The men jumped to their feet and left before they could hear the next count. The prince slammed the door behind them.

"Are you alright?" the prince asked, sheathing his sword.

"I'm fine. Thank you," said the princess, flustered. She looked at the prince for the first time.

"You can see!"

"Yes. It's still just a bit blurry, but I can see much better now."

"Do you know who they were?"

"Probably grave diggers—more like thieves, though. That has been my experience. It is a sordid business that comes with war."

The patients were stirring a bit from all the commotion. Princess Nora began to attend to them.

"Forgive me. I didn't ask your name?" said the prince. "Mine is Frederick. I am an officer of the western realm."

"Yes, I see that."

There was a moment of awkward silence.

"But thank you again for your help—and your protection," Nora sighed.

"The soldiers are doing better."

"I gave them some water last night."

"Thank you. May I ask you a question?"

"Certainly!"

"What did you mean last night when you said, 'mist and sand'?"

The prince was taken aback. He looked out the lone window in the cabin. After a moment's pause, he said, "I've been cursed."

"What do you mean?"

"On the road to the battle front, I was confronted by a hooded man."

"I was too!" gasped Nora.

"You?"

"Yes, the strange man asked me for bread and water."

"Did you give it to him?"

"Yes, though I needed it for the wounded."

"It's good that you did. I refused him." Fredrick looked Nora in the eyes, "That's when he cursed me. He told me that because I was only concerned about the battle, that for the next—what was it, yes—the next twelve days—when I touch food, it will turn to sand, and when I take drink, it will turn to mist. I have tried—unsuccessfully—to drink water and eat food. But it does just as the man said. It turns to mist and sand. I haven't been able to eat anything or drink anything for the last day and a half. And there's more. If anyone assists me with food or drink, the curse will come on them."

"Do you mean that if someone helps you, then they will not be able to eat or drink anything?"

"Yes."

"But will you then be able to eat and drink?"

"Yes, I believe so. But that will never happen." They were both quiet for a moment.

"You must be very thirsty by now."

"It's even in my dreams. It's a funny thing, though. Before this curse, all I could think about was this war. Now it's just wondering how I'm going to stay alive." The prince changed the subject. "But what can we do for these soldiers? Two of them are my men."

"We need to get them to my wagon. We will take them to our hospital."

"Will that be behind your lines?"

"They are not my lines. But, yes, it is."

"That won't do. They will become prisoners. We will return your soldier and we will take the other two to our lines. We will find one of our hospitals and a doctor to treat them."

"He is not *my soldier*," corrected Nora again, "But I suppose they are all my patients—and they will all need constant attention."

"Then you can stay with my men."

"What?" Nora stood with her hands on her hips. "My work is to triage. I am a nurse of the battlefield."

"They will find someone to replace you."

"You are impossible!"

"I am used to giving orders, that's all."

"Not when it comes to my patients!"

"With anything that happens on the battlefield."

"You are so stubborn!"

"But I may have saved your life, you know."

Nora paused, remembering the curse on the officer and all he had done for her and her patients. "We will see," she sighed.

"Good. We will need to find your wagon then. You stay here. I'll have a look around. Don't worry; I won't be too far away."

"If you return to where I was when you first found me on the battlefield, cross the clearing to the northeast—through a wooded area. You should come to a road not too far beyond that. If the nurses' corps can be found, it will be along that road. Be careful, though, there may be pickets."

"That I will," said the prince, closing the door of the cabin behind him. His thirst was becoming an obsession now, but he tried to put it out of his mind by concentrating on his mission. He thought about returning to his command, but the curse cast a different perspective on everything. And, even though he didn't want to admit it, Nora had touched him deeply with her work—healing even in the midst of so much death! There was something to her gracefulness, though, but he couldn't quite put his finger on it.

Returning to the edge of the battlefield, Prince Fredrick carefully surveyed the scene from shadow of a large oak tree. In the distance he could see the gravediggers shoveling a small pit in the ground. He watched as they stripped one of the men of valuables before burying him. Suddenly he heard a twig snap behind him. Turning quickly, he had just enough time to see a rifle butt slam into his forehead.

Chapter 5

When the prince awoke, he was laying on a cot in a small tent with one of his sergeants bending over him.

"You took a good knock from one of my men. They are patrolling the battlefield and are a bit jumpy. My apologies, general. But what brings an officer like you here?"

The prince sat up and gingerly rubbed the bump on his forehead. "It's a long story," he said. "I just can't seem to avoid getting knocked in the head, though. How long was I out?"

"Almost 24 hours. I sent a dispatch to headquarters to let them know we found you. Here, let me get you some coffee," said the sergeant.

"No, no, I'm fine." The prince actually would have loved something to drink—and to eat—but he knew it was futile to try. "I will need several of your men," he said.

"Yes, sir. Of course, sir." There was a slight pause. "But do you mind me asking what you will need them for."

The prince gave the sergeant a look, but then sighed. "I have some wounded men in a cabin not far from here—and one from the eastern army. I made a promise to deliver them to safety."

"This will be dangerous," said the sergeant. "There are enemy patrols everywhere."

"I'm going to propose a truce—under white flag—to clear the dead from the battlefield."

"Yes, sir. I'll make preparations." The sergeant stood and saluted.

The prince stood, but nearly fainted, grasping onto the sergeant's arm.

"Are you alright, sir?"

"I'll be fine. Call your men. And sergeant, I will need food, water and medical supplies—do you have a cart and horses?"

Returning to the battlefield with the supplies and men, the general left his soldiers in the woods and walked out alone into the open with the white flag. It all seemed different now. His soon death seemed to bring everything into focus. He knew the enemy might just shoot him—flag or no flag—after all, a general would be a trophy. About halfway onto the field, the general stopped and raised his white flag above his head. Everything was quiet for a few minutes, and then a lieutenant and two men stepped from the opposite side of the woods and approached him. After some conversation, the men agreed to a temporary truce to bury their dead. The prince also argued for turning the cabin into a battlefield hospital that would be neutral to both sides. The white flag would be planted in the midst of the field and no one would be harmed during the truce. Lastly, he offered to return the wounded soldier to them if they would send their nurses with him to the cabin.

Back with his men, Prince Frederick divided the company between those to help bury the dead and those to go with him to the cabin. He gave special instructions to keep an eye on the grave diggers.

The nurses appeared in due time, led by the lieutenant. One was much older and looked like a member of a religious order—she was probably the most experienced nurse. The other was much younger, and was quick to help with anything needed. The troop followed him with the horse-drawn cart and supplies to the cabin. It was dusk when they arrived. The prince felt very weak now, but was glad to have returned. Princess Nora was standing at the door when they arrived.

"I was afraid you wouldn't return," she said. Then she saw her fellow nurses and rushed to give them a hug. They were quickly looking over the supplies and busying themselves with getting settled.

Prince Frederick dismounted, weak and sore from the day's events. Princess Nora noticed that his forehead and left eye were bruised.

"What happened to you?" asked the princess, reaching gingerly for his face. Her hand touched his cheek with a softness that took the prince by surprise.

"Nothing—it's nothing. I've suffered worse."

"Come inside and rest," said the princess. She took him by the arm. "I was worried about you. Thank you for bringing the supplies and finding the nurses."

"Your soldiers actually found them. You will be glad to know that I negotiated under white flag to turn this cabin into a field hospital for both sides. It will be neutral ground. We won't have to remove the men until they are better."

"That's wonderful news!" said the princess, who stopped and peered into his eyes. "How long has it been—since you had anything to eat or drink?"

"Over two days now," the prince whispered, not wanting everyone to know.

"You cannot go much longer without some nourishment, especially under all this stress."

"Yes, I know. But I am resigned to do what I can—for these men—for you." The prince found himself taking Nora by her shoulders. "You renewed something in me—something for the value and dignity of life. For that I am grateful."

Nora smiled, but her eyes betrayed a deep concern.

The others busied themselves with setting up the hospital and caring for the wounded. One of the soldiers hung a sheet on the outside with the words "Hospital" painted on it. Another built the fire and gathered some wood. As dusk settled, the prince sent the soldiers back to their company with instructions to bring any other wounded they found and a regular supply of medicines, bandages, food and water.

The older nurse noticed how Nora and the general stayed close to each other. She could tell by the way Nora touched him that there was something more to their relationship. She expected the general to be barking orders, but instead, there was kindness in his speech and softness in the way he treated the men. When everyone ate the rations, she also noticed that the general took nothing. Soon the group settled down for the night.

At daylight Nora awoke to the sound of Prince Frederick moaning for water. *He must be dreaming*, she thought. She knew what she had to do. Taking his head in her arms, she tilted it up and gave the prince some water to drink. He had taken several gulps before he realized what had happened. Knocking the cup from her hands, he cried, "No, no, you can't—no, the curse will be on you!" It was too late; the prince felt as though a dark cloud had lifted from him.

Chapter 6

Nora picked up the cup. "It's what I must do," she said. "You are one of my patients now. I would give my life for the care of any of them."

Even so, she felt a sense of darkness envelop her.

Hearing the commotion, the nurses were soon surrounding them. The older nurse was the first to speak. "What's going on?"

"Nora gave me something to drink," said Frederick, sitting up.

The nurses looked at each other, expecting something else.

Frederick noticed that Nora had tears in her eyes and took her hand.

"I'm sorry I raised my voice. I just didn't want to see you hurt."

She nodded.

"Can someone tell us what is *really* going on?" said the older nurse.

Prince Frederick explained everything. "Nora caught me off guard when she gave me something to drink. Now it seems that she has saved me— but at the cost of her own life."

"This is all very strange," said the younger nurse.

Everyone was silent for a minute. Nora tried to drink something and watched the water swirl into mist.

Then the older nurse spoke. "I know where you can find bread and drink that no curse can command."

"Where?" asked the prince and princess almost in unison.

"It was nourishment born out of a curse—out of taking all curses to be more precise. You must trust me on this. Here's what you must do. There is a chapel three day's journey from here. Take the north road into the mountains until you come to an old oak tree—larger than you have ever seen before. Take the fork to the right. You will find a small stone chapel at its end. The door is always open. In the chapel you will find a table that is set each day with bread and a cup. There is no curse that can prevent you from taking from these."

"You must go!" said the young nurse. "We can handle things here."

"Take some food and a canteen with you, young man," said the older nurse. "And here eat an apple now for your strength. No wonder you looked so pale. And go. Go! Don't delay!" She gave Nora a warm hug and sent them on their way. "And may God go with you!"

Both nurses said a quick prayer as they rode off.

Prince Frederick took a route skirting his lines and avoiding the enemy— quietly riding around some pickets guarding the road. There was a truce, but he didn't want to take any chances. Once completely clear of the battlefield, they found the north road and journeyed until nightfall. It was a cool evening, so the prince prepared a fire. It felt good to take food and drink, but he felt uncomfortable doing so in front of Nora.

"Please, go right ahead," said Nora. "I'm glad you can eat and drink now."

"I wish I had responded to that strange man differently," said the prince. "But then we would have never met. And now there is a hospital for both armies—that would not have happened, either. It seems fate has brought us together. And thank you for your help."

"It's you I have to thank. To tell you the truth, I've wanted to end this war for a long time. But I could only think of fighting harder to bring our victory—to end it that way. But you've shown me another way."

"I know you're a general, but how much can you really do to actually end the war?"

Prince Frederick was quiet for a moment. "I have a confession to make. I am King William's son."

Nora gasped. "You are *Prince* Frederick! Then you really could make a difference." She looked away—angry for a moment, but then remembered that he was doing all of this for her. She wondered whether she could trust him completely, then confessed, "There is something I need to tell you as well. I am Princess Nora, King Edward's daughter."

"No—what? Really? That explains it."

"Explains what?"

"Your gracefulness. You do not act like a commoner. Only someone trained at the court would act as you do. But a nurse? How did you convince your father to become a nurse?"

"It wasn't easy. But I think I'm as stubborn as you are." Nora smiled.

The prince was quiet again. He had a fleeting thought that as his prisoner, he could use Nora to bring the eastern kingdom into submission. But Nora had saved his life—and he was now feeling much more for her. He reached for Nora's hand. "I'm sorry for what has happened to you. I hope your nurse friend was right. I hope this will work out."

"It will," said Nora. But she had doubts. Even so, being with Prince Frederick gave her an unusual peace.

From daybreak they rode hard through the second day, but Prince Frederick slowed the pace on the third day—Nora was visibly tired from not eating or drinking and riding so long. They eventually came to a large oak standing between two roads forking to the left and right, just as the old nurse had said. It was dawn of the third day.

Chapter 7

The chapel was unassuming, made of wood and stone, but did have a steeple and some stain glass windows. Just as the nurse had said, the front doors were open. Prince Frederick dismounted and helped Nora off her horse. She was very weak, so the prince decided to pick her up and carry her up the stairs and through the doors of the chapel. Setting her down, they looked around. There were candles and light coming through the stain glass that illumined the chapel room. There were several rows of pews facing the front. The sunlight shone through a large stain glass cross in the back window and lit up a table in front of it. There was a plate of bread and a cup on it—also just as the nurse had said.

"I haven't been in one of these in a long time," said the prince.

"Attending chapel was a requirement in nurses training," said Nora. "I actually found a lot of comfort in the prayers."

"There's the bread and drink. Do you want to try it?"

"Yes. But give me a moment. I want to give thanks first." Nora walked to the front and sat on the pew. She bowed her head.

The prince felt out of place and remained in the back of the chapel. He looked around. *Someone has to take care of this*, he thought.

Nora stood and walked to the table and broke a piece off the loaf. It almost glistened in the light.

The prince finally walked to the front. Nora looked up at the prince with a questioning look in her eyes. "Go ahead. We've come a long way and we can't turn back now," said the prince, placing his arm around her shoulder.

Nora took a bite and tasted the sweetness of the bread in her mouth. Her eyes swelled with tears. Then she took a drink from the cup and swallowed down several gulps. Expecting wine, she was surprised that it was simply juice—but far more refreshing. She also felt a darkness lift from her—the curse had been broken as well!

"It's gone," said Princess Nora.

"You were able to eat and drink," observed the prince as he wiped tears from her cheeks.

"Yes and the curse has lifted. I feel as though a weight has lifted from me."

"Your nurse was right, then. In the Eucharist no curse can remain."

They embraced—relieved and glad to be free again.

"All our lives are as mist and sand," said a voice from back of the chapel. Princess Nora and Prince Frederick turned to see a man standing in the doorway. The prince immediately recognized the man who had stopped him on the road days before. He reached for his sword, but Nora's hand stopped him.

"Have you come to curse us again?" said the prince.

"You were already under a curse," said the strange man. "I simply brought out into the natural realm what was happening to you spiritually. It was destroying both kingdoms. Only when you learned to serve each other did you find an end to your strife. And only when you found your way to this table did you find the solution to war—to man's inhumanity to man. It was a necessary evil to break your focus on the things of this war."

"Who are you?" asked the princess. "Are you the chaplain here?"

"I am the caretaker of this place."

"You said once that my father may have caused our wars. What did you mean?"

"Long ago I served your father when both kingdoms were at peace. He trusted my advice and used to come frequently to this sacred place. But the cares of this world pulled him away more and more, until he came no longer. One day he made a promise to provide needed food to King William—for his kingdom was suffering from a famine. He traded for the rich lands of the valley which had been shared by both kingdoms. But there was no compassion or generosity in his heart. I found him and confronted him for his hardness of heart. But he refused my advice—his pride and greed had twisted his heart. That's when he banished me. When the western kingdom again ran out of food, and the farming of the valley was lost to them, the wars began. Now you see—only if the two of you could be brought together would there be a chance to end this conflict. But you also had to see your own need—your need for what this table has to offer."

The prince turned back to look at the bread and cup.

"They represent the body and blood of One who died for all the hard hearts of this world," continued the caretaker. "Those who partake of them, receive the life he gave—and never thirst or hunger again."

"Then let me take this as well," said the prince. He knelt before the table, prayed and took the bread and cup.

When he rose from the table, the prince and princess looked at each other deeply. The prince turned to the caretaker.

"I have a task for you."

The caretaker smiled.

"I want you to take my signet ring and a letter to my parents and bring them here."

The princess understood him immediately. "Yes, and I will write one as well. They should make a truce—just like the one made by Prince Frederick. Once they are here, we must make them end this war."

"It will not be easy," said the prince. "But I know a way that will convince them—and make me the happiest man on earth." Prince Frederick took Princess Nora by the hands and knelt before her. "Ever since I met you, you captured my heart—with your gracefulness and kindness—not only did you save my life, but you healed something broken deep within me. I can't imagine living without you. Will you do me the honor of taking my hand in marriage?"

Both families received the letters with great surprise but set aside their differences for their children's welfare. They gathered at the chapel for the wedding that not only united two in deep love, but also ended once for all the wars between the kingdoms. Soon the wedding bells rang throughout the land

.

And yes, they all lived happily ever after.

Broken Shepherd

Sit here. Recount the past with me.

You smile, but the wounds through the Spirit check.

Press hard-heavy from each word,

As weighted hands upon my breast.

Expectations!

So many were the plans you laid,

Unrealized, now abandoned.

Held in your eyes,

Like floods damned up by walls,

Too strong to breach.

Limitations!

My shepherd friend, you led to rest.

But crags and thorns of another way,

Tore scars you could not heal.

The way, so clear before, was now,

A way that leads to death.

Demands!

Too many, many matters pressed,
Sweet presence from your life.
The past was now a bitter taste.
As hard and hurt, and cynical,
Were the flavors of your heart.

Now carefully,
Now quietly my answer,
As arms around your heart,
Gave comfort from the Comforter,
By directing you to rest.

Your passion came from music,
From the joy-strands of your heart.
Turn again and find praise-pasture,
The place of your repose.

The Shepherd now has sought for you,
And seeks to bear you home.

Uncle Bob and the Great White Van

After moving up from Florida to be a part of our church, Uncle Bob moved into a little side room off the converted car port in our house. Bob was a short, wiry red head with a strong, carpenter-built frame. He wasn't really our uncle, but the kids called him that as a sort-of unofficial family title. But the thing that stood out the most about Uncle Bob was his white van.

I think it was a remnant from the "Hippy" days, except that the flowers had long since been painted over. It had a rag for a gas cap, which hung out like a Molotov cocktail begging to explode and put it out of its misery. (I had threatened to light it.) The driver's side window was busted out (from trying to close a stubborn door), but that was ok, because a thick cloud of blue and green exhaust fumes continually surrounded the van while it was running—in and out—and the open window provided some much needed ventilation. (The other windows had long since ceased to roll down.) You could always tell when Uncle Bob was coming down the road since all the wildlife scattered for miles around.

I made the mistake once (and only once) of riding with Bob in the van. When I opened the side door, I quickly realized that there was no passenger seat—only a large box of carpenter nails—an *open* box of carpenter nails—for a seat. When I sat gingerly on it, I was so far down that I couldn't see over the dash. But, again, that really didn't matter because you could watch the road go by through the gaping holes in the floor.

The tires on the van were as bald as you can get and still hold air. (They looked more like inner tubes.) But Bob didn't drive much in the rain, since carpenters don't work on rainy days. But I remember one cold, winter morning, about 5 a.m., when Uncle Bob needed to get to a job. It started with a "whreeek…bang!" Bob was trying to close the driver's door. "Whreeek…bang!" Still not closed. "Whreeek…(there was a long pause) BANG!" That time it closed.

Now came the hard part—starting the engine. There was the whining, grinding ignition, then the long chuga, chuga, chuga, CHUGA, CHUGA, CHUGA, backfire, cough, sputter. Try again. By this time, Kim and I are sitting up in bed. Come on, Bob, you can get it going. CHUGA, CHUGA, CHUGA, CHUGA, CHUGA, VROOOOM! Green and blue exhaust clouded the windows outside our bedroom.

(Now maybe we can go back to sleep. Nope, too soon.) Ice had covered the driveway during the night, and Bob's van was parked down the slope at the end of the driveway. The next thing we heard was the sound of violent spinning: vvvvvvvmmmm. Vvvvvvvvvvvvvvvvvvmmmm. VVVVVVVVVVVVVVVVVVVmmmmm. Up and down the slope the white van spun its slick tires, trying to grip something to help it get to the top, each time getting a bit closer to the goal, blue smoke filling the air. (By this time I wondered if the neighbors were rooting him on as well.) Finally, we could hear him at the top—off he went. (But no chance now for sleeping.)

Bob warned the kids that the van had a mind of its own—a sort of *sadistic* mind of its own, I had interjected. If it saw the kid's toys left out on the driveway, it just jerked the steering wheel out of Bob's hands to run over them. If you leave stuff out, he couldn't be responsible for the actions of the van. Besides, he had warned the kids many times not to leave toys out on the driveway. (I guess that's why there was such a wobble when Bobbie rode his bike.)

Well, one day Uncle Bob was sitting in his van at the end of the driveway filling out some paperwork and getting ready to go to his next job. Finally ready, he started the van and began backing up. Clank! Bob had backed into something—probably Bobbie's bike again, or so he thought. Now, you have to understand. This van doesn't have any outside mirrors and the inside one is blocked from tools and such in the back of the van. Well, Bobbie shouldn't park his bike behind the van, so Uncle Bob let the van roll forward a bit, and then he backed up again. Bam! Wait, this wasn't a bike. Uncle Bob jumped out of the van, and, sure enough, some friends had parked their station wagon behind the van. And there in the front seat was the friend's wife—her mouth wide open! Bob had hit the car twice!

One day Uncle Bob was driving down the highway when he prayed, "Lord, when it's time to get a new van, just let me know." Within seconds the engine seized and the van rolled to a stop.

There was rejoicing in the whole neighborhood.

Uncle Bob and the Pillar of Fire

When Uncle Bob lived with us, the neighborhood that was largely populated by Asians. They often loved to sit on their porches as dusk gathered, chatting loudly in their native language—quite foreign to us—and cooking their dinner meals on little hibachis. Every now and then you could see the flames pop up as they cooked. I often wondered if they had a competition going among them to see who could get the flames to leap the highest.

One late afternoon my mother dropped by our house and, after parking her car in our driveway, thought it would be nice to check if we had picked up our mail yet. However, when she reached for the mailbox, she was immediately stung on her right thumb by a black wasp. She rushed into the house complaining about her pain and displaying her wound for everyone to see. One look from my wife, and I knew I would have to do something about it. After all, killing bugs is the man's responsibility. Pondering who had made up *that* rule, I walked out to the mailbox and carefully examined the bushes that surrounded it. Whoa! There it was—one of the largest paper wasp nests I had ever seen! No wonder mom got stung. (And this wouldn't be a very friendly welcome to the local postal workers.)

Well, to handle any problem, there are three things that guys need: duct tape, WD 40, and gasoline. Yup, gasoline will do just fine for this. But I couldn't do this alone; I would need Uncle Bob's help to pull this off. Timing *is* everything here. You don't want to stir wasps up by gassing their nest unless you can light it up at the same time.

I got Bob and we came up with this plan (not exactly approved by your local fire marshal): I would put the gas in a pan, run up and dowse the nest, and take off down the driveway. He would follow behind, lighting a match and throwing it on the nest. (Profoundly simple, but I wasn't about to throw that match.)

It was getting dusk by now. I donned a sweatshirt with a hood and some large oven gloves (those little pests weren't getting me!) and filled the pan with gas. Bob tore a match out of the matchbook and followed me outside.

Ready? Yup.

Now here's where everything seemed to move in slow motion, though it only took a few seconds. I ran up to the nest and dowsed it as planned, but when Bob came behind me, he couldn't get the match to light. Once, twice, three times he struck it—and nothing. Ok, try another match. Come on, Bob. There are a lot of angry wasps in there. Ah, there it lit.

As Bob tossed the match, it seemed to drift end over end in some surreal time warp. Then, WHOMP! Before it even hit the nest, the paper exploded into a pillar of fire that burst fifteen feet in the air, burning out all the bushes around it and licking the leaves in the magnolia tree above it. I felt the explosion against my chest and stood in awe at the torch we had created.

Then I heard all my neighbors exclaiming something as they pointed in shock at the pillar of fire. But I didn't need to speak their language to know what they must have said, "That's the biggest hibachi flame ever!"

Devotions for His Presence

Day 1

I have been crucified with Christ and I no longer live, but Christ lives in me. The life I live in the body, I live by faith in the Son of God, who loved me and gave himself for me.
—Galatians 2:20

George Mueller once wrote:

"There was a day when I died:

- Died to George Mueller: to his tastes, his opinions, his preferences and his will.

- Died to the world—its approval or censure.

- Died to the approval or blame even of my brethren and friends.

"Since then I have studied to only show myself approved unto God."

How foreign this is to us today—with all our approval ratings and polls! We boast of only seeking the approval of God, yet we relish the handclapping and pats on the back. Success is measured in numbers!

Yes, Christ had the crowds follow Him, waving the palm branches or eating the loaves and fishes. But more than once He confronted them with hard questions, or drove them away with difficult statements. He didn't win friends by challenging, "You are looking for me…because you ate the loaves and had your fill." He only gained enemies by commanding them to eat His flesh and drink His blood. In the end they played the part of all crowds, leaving Him for His offense. Gleeful to turn on Him. Abandoning Him to suffer. Leaving Him alone in the tomb.

Have we really died to the impulse of the crowd? Do we know how to stand when all others move on? No cry of the crowd, no shout of the multitude, no roar of the throng means as much as these simple words from the only important One, "Well done, good and faithful servant." Is anything as important as the approval of the Lord?

Come, Lord, and nail me to the cross.

Prayer Topics: Death and Life in Christ; Standing Alone; Approval and Rejection.

Day 2

David wrote in one of his Psalms:

> *One thing I ask of the LORD,*
> *this is what I seek:*
> *that I may dwell in the house of the LORD*
> *all the days of my life,*
> *to gaze upon the beauty of the LORD*
> *and to seek him in his temple.*—Ps. 27:4

David sought the Lord's glory during his life as the singular cry of his heart. Yet, despite all the majesty that may have emanated from the tabernacle, the glory David gazed upon could not have compared to the surpassing glory revealed to the three disciples at Christ's transfiguration. The glory of the old—the law, the patriarchs, and the covenants—the glory found on Mt. Sinai—was fading before the glory on the new mount. For each miracle of Christ manifested His glory— veiled though it was in flesh—the glory of the Kingdom of Heaven breaking into this age. And His crucifixion displayed His glory despite such staggering suffering. For herein lies the greatest honor, the greatest demonstration of glory: to sacrifice oneself that the will of the Father may be done.

Shall the disciple's path not pass through Gethsemane?

"One thing I ask, this is what I seek…" Is it His presence that we seek above all else? Can we like Moses refuse to go any further without His presence? To preach or teach without His anointing? To minister without first having gazed upon His beauty in prayer? Without first worshipping Him in the corporate gathering?

"One thing I ask, this is what I seek…" Has David's cry become the cry of our hearts? Or are we distracted by "the cares of this life and the deceitfulness of riches?" What one thing can we declare to be the purpose of our life?

Prayer Topics: Desire for Him; A Singular Heart; Praise during Suffering; The Cares of this Life; Draw Near to God.

Day 3

I want to know Christ and the power of his resurrection and the fellowship of sharing in his sufferings, becoming like him in his death, and so, somehow, to attain to the resurrection from the dead.—
Philippians 3:10

The pursuit of Christ is the goal of every Christian.

That we can come before Him to delight in His presence is guaranteed by the trail He blazed before us into the heavenlies. There we can kneel with Him in quiet intercession or listen as He gently whispers a word of wisdom or a word of knowledge or a prophecy that we might continue His ministry on earth. There we become more like Him—for only as we are with Him do we learn to be like Him.

That we must share in His pain is the duty of every disciple, and the common result of every person who has heard His compassionate heart groan for the lost, suffering and dying.

That we long for the power of His resurrection is right and proper. That we possess it is the inheritance of all who believe—for He *is* the Resurrection and the Life.

But resurrection always follows suffering and compassion. Even as Christ was about to raise His friend, Lazarus, from the grave, He was twice deeply moved—even to the point of tears. Oh, how we want to be like Him in His power! But how few pay the price to be like Him in His death!

Prayer Topics: Christlikeness; Listen for His Heart; Groaning with Him; Compassion; Weeping.

Day 4

I will betroth you to me forever; I will betroth you in righteousness and justice, in love and compassion. I will betroth you in faithfulness, and you will acknowledge the LORD. "In that day I will respond," declares the LORD... "I will show my love..."

—Hosea 2:19-21, 23

God is a God who responds. He watches over us; He listens to us; He moves on our behalf. The Lord declared, "In that day I will respond." But what day? Under what circumstances does He respond? It is the day of betrothal for marriage—the day of covenant and intimacy with God. It is His Bride that He hears—His Bride that He dotes over, listens to, caresses, seeks out, longs for.

How interesting it is that God promises on this day to pay a bridal price! What is the bridal price He promises? It is righteousness, justice, love and compassion. It is covenant relationship. When God married His people, the bridal price He paid was a promise of relationship based on these four critically important relational terms: righteousness, justice, love and compassion. For the marriage covenant is not just a contract, nor an agreement involving monetary payment, but rather, it is a deep, abiding relationship. Isn't it interesting that we think of a bridal price in terms of monetary compensation? But God thinks first in terms of relationship.

If these four terms are essential ingredients in God's marital relationship with His people, then these four terms are integral to any marital covenant relationship. They demonstrate more than any other terms the way a husband should treat his wife.

Among these four relationship gifts promised by our Bridegroom, one word stands out. It is the Hebrew word "hesed." This word means a loyal love—a kind of steadfast, devoted love that forms the bond of covenant relationship—an indissoluble relationship no matter the failures or unfaithfulness of the spouse.

Covenant love demands commitment and loyalty. Without that loyal love, there can be no intimate relationship, for covenant relationship requires an unconditional trust. When trust is established through commitment and loyalty, then relationship results. The deeper the commitment and trust, the deeper the relationship becomes.

This is what God means when He says He will show His love. He is eternally faithful. He is eternally loyal. He will never compromise His fidelity to the covenant. In Hosea's prophetic words, and in the prophetic example of his own marriage, we find the kind of love every bridegroom should emulate!

Prayer Topics: Covenant Relationship; God Shows His Love; God Responds; Righteousness, Justice, Love and Compassion; Loyalty; Marriage.

Day 5

> *The LORD replied, "My Presence will go with you,*
> *and I will give you rest."*
> *Then Moses said to him, "If your Presence does not go with us, do not*
> *send us up from here. How will anyone know that you are pleased with*
> *me and with your people unless you go with us? What else will*
> *distinguish me and your people from all the other people on the face of*
> *the earth?"*—Exodus 33:14-15

"Bend us, Lord!"—Evan Roberts, Welsh Revivalist

What distinguishes us from everyone else? Moses understood that His Presence in us, leading us, guiding us, changing us, meant all the difference. Whatever the endeavor might be, we need His Presence in it. And if we need His presence in our day-to-day walk, how much more do we need it in our corporate worship!

How often in the West the focus of worship becomes entertainment, or production, or performance! Too often the Church has focused on all the cultural trappings that attract the crowds and too little on what it takes to hear from the Spirit. It has become program based, not Presence based. The Spirit is corralled into time limits, or after-glow meetings, or altar prayers, or anything that doesn't cause a disturbance. But shouldn't "Disturb us, God!" be the cry of our hearts? Where is the revived heart that longs to be bent by the Spirit? Do we make Him instead the great, domesticated One?

Supposing Jesus walked into a Sunday service in a typical American church. Would He be told, "Wait! Sit back here. Don't say anything; we've got our schedule to keep…?" Would we allow His interruption?

Would we allow Him to speak? Certainly we would! Yet every Sunday in churches all over America, we say the same squelching things to the Spirit. When He comes, shall He not have expression? Should we not, in fact, sit at His feet and hear what is on His heart?

It was a great disturbance at Pentecost when the Spirit fell like tongues of fire (Acts 2:1-4). It was a great disturbance when the disciples prayed and the place was shaken as they were filled with the Spirit (Acts 4:31). Even in the one record of a service in the New Testament the unbeliever was so disturbed in his heart because of the prophetic word that falling down and worshipping he exclaimed, "God is really among you!" (1 Corinthians 14:25). Instead we pamper visitors.

Where is the prophetic word? Where is the conviction? The power? The challenge? The disturbance?

How greatly Moses understood! "If your Presence does not go with us, do not send us up from here." If His Presence isn't in the twenty minutes we worship, why do we stop? If His Presence is driven from the service, why do we even gather? What is more important than His Presence? What have we settled for?

Prayer Topics: Presence; Guidance; Witness of the Spirit; True Worship; Revived Heart; Bending in His Presence; "Disturb us, God!"

Day 6

"Woe is me, for I am undone!"—Isaiah 6:5

When Simon Peter saw this, he fell at Jesus' knees and said, "Go away from me, Lord; I am a sinful man!" For he and all his companions were astonished at the catch of fish they had taken."—Luke 5:8-9

The Book of Isaiah describes how the prophet is ushered into the Divine Court and witnesses scenes so awesome it leaves him undone. There he is commissioned to prophesy the lawsuits of the court to a recalcitrant people.

Peter witnesses the miraculous catch of fish and falls at the feet of Christ begging Him to leave. There he is commissioned to "catch men" instead.

God shook both men to the core of their being by an encounter with His power and presence. That shaking must precede any commissioning. For the purpose of commissioning is to shake a world hardened by sin. And any commissioning that lacks such an encounter will not long endure the obstinate hearts of humankind, and will, in fact be blunted and dulled by its constant resistance.

Any true encounter with God will do these two things: it will leave you broken by His power and stirred to do His bidding. You cannot have a real encounter with His presence and remain the same.

Like Jacob wrestling with the messenger of God, you will come away with a limp and a blessing. You arrive as Jacob at Jabbok, but leave as Israel from Peniel.

A bush that burned unending turned aside a different shepherd. But the presence and power of God commissioned him with holy apostolic fire— a fire that ignited a people and seared the heart of Pharaoh.

"Woe is me, for I am undone!" Has an encounter with Christ left you echoing the prophet's words? If not, then perhaps it is time to turn aside and wrestle with God.

Prayer Topics: Prophetic Lawsuits; Seeking His Presence; Wrestling with God; Commissioning; Shaking the World.

Day 7

Look! There he stands behind our wall, gazing through the windows,
peering through the lattice. My lover spoke and said to me, "Arise, my
darling, my beautiful one, and come with me."—Song 2:9-10

There are times when Christ seems to hide from us—in almost playfulness—watching to see if we are looking—watching to see if we desire Him. Do you see His smile? Does your heart not leap within you?

We erect the walls that separate us from enjoying His presence—walls of rebellion—lattices of selfishness. But He sees right through them. He knows how to get around them!

Could we not find Him? He will find us, taking us by the hand, and drawing us to follow Him. This is the Bridegroom who comes for His Bride. His heart is filled with encouraging words, loving words, reassuring words that draw us into intimacy.

How will we respond on the Day He comes? Will He find us too busy, too self-absorbed, too deep in the things of this world? Like Lot's wife, our attention is elsewhere. Or do we delight in finding Him? Do we wait at the door with extra oil, knowing the cry will yet be heard, "The Bridegroom comes!"?

Our God is the God who comes. At the intersection of heaven and earth, you can find Him. When the Spirit beckons, you can find Him. Do you see His smile? Then take off the bridal shoes and run after Him. He is your beloved and you are His.

Prayer Topics: Seeking and Finding Christ; Delighting in Christ; Intimacy; Turning Toward God; Bride and Groom; Second Coming.

Day 8

> But as for me, my feet had almost slipped;
>
> I had nearly lost my foothold.
>
> For I envied the arrogant
>
> when I saw the prosperity of the wicked.
>
> When I tried to understand all this,
>
> it was oppressive to me
>
> till I entered the sanctuary of God;
>
> then I understood their final destiny.

—Psalm 73:2-3, 16-17

It is not unusual for the wicked to prosper in this age. In fact, despite the plethora of laws and regulations to constrain evil, the wicked still seem to find ways to circumvent society's restraints and exploit others for gain. And they seem to do it with ease, without remorse, without regret—callous in all their ways.

Psalm 73 reveals the struggle of Asaph when he was tempted to envy the prosperity of the wicked. At first he recounts how all the outward appearances seemed to confirm their success. They looked happy and prosperous—"free from the burdens common to man." For a moment the prideful triumphs of the wicked captivated the heart of the psalmist. How his own righteous acts seemed to pale in comparison to the achievements of the wicked!

Until he entered the presence of the Lord.

There is something about the presence of the Lord that brings everything into proper perspective. His presence brings judgment back into view. His presence reminds us that this age is temporary—that it will be engulfed by eternity. His presence reminded Asaph of the wicked's final destiny.

"What good will it be for a man if he gains the whole world, yet forfeits his soul?"

Without His presence, we too may be overcome by the temptations of this age. But whenever our feet slip after the wicked, His presence is there to point us to truth. His presence will cause us to conclude along with Asaph: "Earth has nothing I desire besides you!"

Prayer Topics: Seeking His Presence; Desiring Him Above All Else; Contentment; Final Judgment; Eternity.

Day 9

"Oh, that you would rend the heavens and come down, that the mountains would tremble before you! As when fire sets twigs ablaze and causes water to boil, come down to make your name known to your enemies and cause the nations to quake before you!"
—Isaiah 64:1-2

"The god who answers by fire, he is God!"—1 Kings 18:24

"I have come to send fire on the earth, and how I wish it were already kindled!"—Luke 12:49

When God comes—when His presence invades the sphere of our existence—He comes by fire. And it is fire that revives us. In simplest terms, *revival is fire*. It is an intense, spiritual fire that burns deep and prolonged. It will scorch before it heals. It will ruin us before it changes us.

But fire doesn't fall on an empty altar. If there is no humility, no brokenness, no prayer and fasting, no conviction of sin, no spirit of expectation, no *sacrifice*, fire will not fall! But for those who pay the price, His presence will come like fire:

- *It burns.* The fire of God burns away the chaff—the worthless sin-burdens that cling to us, and hinder the pure wheat of God's Word from nourishing us. We are a culture entertained, but bored; wealthy with materialism, but poor in the true riches; full of knowledge, but empty of truth. It is only the fire of God that can turn this nation around.

- *It purifies.* The fire of God separates the holy from the unholy. It melts away the dross of this world. It refines us into the pure image of Christ.

- *It softens.* The fire of God reduces even the hardest hearts to the soft, pliable material for God's shaping. When God comes, He softens the hard crust that encases our hearts. Like wax before a fire, God mollifies and tenderizes us for His work.

- *It warms.* The fire of God creates in us such a presence of God that the world will be attracted to us—they are like men and women in spiritual winter—unsaved—who are drawn to the warmth of God's presence.

- *It glows.* The light of God's fire breaks into the darkness of this world. Darkness must flee; it can never overcome the light!

- *It spreads.* Just one spark of revival can set a nation on fire. Soon the newly saved will pass the fire of revival from one to another, spreading it across this nation.

- *It tempers.* Through the constant heating and re-heating and watering and hammering of the Spirit, our character is formed and shaped into His image.

How does God answer our sacrifice? He answers by fire!

Prayer Topics: Revival; Fire of God's Presence; Sacrifice; Applying Spiritual Disciplines; Christlikeness.

Day 10

When you ascended on high, you led captives in your train; you received
gifts from men, even from the rebellious—that you, O LORD God
might dwell there.—Ps. 68:18

The Psalmist recounts the occasion at mount Sinai when the Levites were
separated from among the children of Israel by the Lord and then given
back to Aaron and his sons to help serve at the Tabernacle (Nu. 8:6, 11-
19; 18:6; cf. Ex. 32:17-26). Numbers records how, while the rest of Israel
held to their rebellion and lasciviousness, the Levites rallied to Moses.
That day, the Lord took the Levites and set them apart to serve at the
Tabernacle—the meeting place of God and Israel.

From the account in Numbers, we should note that ministers:

1. Must stand with the Lord (even against the crowd).

2. Must be first captured by the Lord (the captives are the gifts).

3. Are given wholly to the Lord.

4. Are then given by God as gifts to serve the people.

When describing the ministries that Christ bestowed on His Body to
serve it and bring the members into maturity, Paul looks back at this
Psalm and its antecedent in Numbers to describe five types of ministers
as gifts. This time Paul refers to Christ's ascension, which the Sinai
account prefigures.

"When he ascended on high, he led captives in his train and gave gifts to
men."

...It was he who gave some to be apostles, some to be prophets, some to
be evangelists, and some to be pastors and teachers, to prepare God's

people for works of service, so that the body of Christ may be built up until we all reach unity in the faith and in the knowledge of the Son of God and become mature, attaining to the whole measure of the fullness of Christ.—Ephesians 4:8, 11-13

The gifts are the ministers. But how do we treat these gifts? Do we leave them unwrapped and unappreciated? Do we just stare at them and admire the paper and bows? Or do we receive the gifts, unwrap them and allow the gifts to bring us joy?

Further, we must not forget, that the whole purpose for bestowing these grace-gifts was that God "might dwell there" (Ps. 68:18)! Just as the Levites supported the work of the ministry at the Tabernacle in the wilderness—the dwelling place of God, so ministers today serve the Body for the purpose of God dwelling among them.

Unfortunately, many performance-oriented churches today focus on the service as the means of attracting and keeping members, resulting in leaders who are good at entertaining, but not at releasing the Spirit. As a result, the Church has lost the art of discipling and building real community which these gift-ministries provide, thus limiting the movement of God's presence. But when the Church becomes a business, it prostitutes the Bride.

May God's ministers never forget that they are grace-filled gifts, captured by God's heart and then given to lead the people of God into His presence—that they may reach "the whole measure of the fullness of Christ."

Prayer Topics: Presence of God; Ministers of God; Receiving Ministry; Core Values of the Church; Maturity in Christ.

Day 11

> Today you are driving me from the land,
>
> and I will be hidden from your presence;
>
> I will be a restless wanderer on the earth..."—Cain, Ge. 4:16

> "Thou hast made us for thyself, O Lord, and our hearts are restless until they find their rest in thee."—St. Augustine

Part of the judgment against Cain's vicious murder of his brother, Abel, was to be cast from the presence of the Lord and become a restless wanderer on the earth. Whatever presence of God that remained after the banishment from Eden was now taken from Cain—a punishment he declared to be too much for him.

How sin robs us of the precious fellowship with our Lord!

All humankind now reaps the consequence of sin: a restless heart—an insatiable longing so deep and so disturbing that we can only be called vagabonds—until we fall helplessly into the arms of our Savior, our Prince of Peace.

The saddest day in the history of the nation of Israel was the day the presence of God lifted up from the Temple of Jerusalem and departed. Ezekiel looked in the Spirit and watched God's majestic glory leave (Ezek. 10). The recalcitrant sin of the nation had driven Him away! The harlot had conceived an Ichabod—"the glory has departed" (1 Sa. 4:21). Can we expect anything less in a nation that has murdered so many innocent unborn? May God not so deal with us!

Sam Storm wrote, "We must swallow up the flicker of sin's pleasure in the forest fire of holy satisfaction. The only thing that will ultimately break the power of sin is passion for Jesus. The only thing that will guard me from being entrapped by sin is being entranced by Jesus."

This nation wants our prophets to prophesy "pleasant things" (IS. 30:10), but the message must echo the decrees from the Court of Heaven. Who will be a voice against the sin of this nation? Who will be the guide to lead us to the rest found only in Christ?

Prayer Topics: Repentance for Sin; Deliverance from Abortion; Restoration of a Godly Nation; Passion for Christ.

Day 12

> Then a great and powerful wind tore the mountains apart
>
> and shattered the rocks before the Lord,
>
> but the Lord was not in the wind.
>
> After the wind there was an earthquake,
>
> but the Lord was not in the earthquake.
>
> After the earthquake came a fire,
>
> but the Lord was not in the fire.
>
> And after the fire came a gentle whisper.

Have you ever been in a cave—a dark place separate from regular community—sometimes a place of loneliness, despair and dejection? Moses, David, and Daniel were all in caves at one point in their lives. And so was the prophet Elijah.

Even after Elijah's defeat of the 450 prophets of Baal on Mt. Carmel—a spectacular victory over idolatry—he faced the recalcitrant King Ahab and the hatred of Queen Jezebel. Feeling alone and unable to affect lasting change, Elijah flees south through Israel, Judah, and into the desert. Sustained twice by the angel of the Lord, Elijah travels 40 days to the cave at Mt. Sinai to await God's presence.

It's not uncommon for a "mountaintop" experience to be followed by a "valley." You can serve God spectacularly, and still be rejected. In fact, Elijah was ready to turn in his prophet's badge and write his resignation: "I have had enough, Lord…" Have you ever felt that way? Have you lost a job? A ministry? A church? A loved one?

It is often in times of disappointment and rejection—even depression—that we see our needs the most. And just as the angel told Elijah that the journey was too much for him, so life's trials are too much for us without God's help—without His grace.

But notice how God was with Elijah all along! Even when we aren't exactly following His will, He's there. And in the depths of despair, He doesn't burst upon us like wind, an earthquake, or fire—but in a gentle voice. God's presence isn't just in the spectacular.

God was there in the cave with Elijah. And He will not abandon you.

Prayer Topics: Comfort in Suffering; Release from Depression; How to Minister to Others

About the Author

Alicia has always been fascinated by the macabre. She devoured Stephen King novels and horror movies from a young age, eventually leading to her writing her own horror novel after years of hard work and dedication.

When Alicia isn't immersed in her writing, she finds joy in her other passions. These include reading and listening to classic rock music, which inspired this book. Her home library is a sanctuary where she can often be found, either reading or listening to her record collection. Alicia lives with her loving husband, Michael, and their four-legged family members: three cats named Ozzy, Elton, and Axl and their dog, Dolly.

Alicia is thrilled to share her love for horror with readers through her debut novel, *Psychosomatic Slaughter,* and hopes to establish herself as a unique voice in the horror genre.

Author Photo By Lexi Harner